BRAMARD'S CASE

Also by Davide Longo in English translation

The Last Man Standing

DAVIDE LONGO

BRAMARD'S CASE

Translated from the Italian by
Silvester Mazzarella

MACLEHOSE PRESS
QUERCUS · LONDON

First published in the Italian language as *Il Caso Bramard*
By Giangiacomo Feltrinelli Editore, Milano, 2014
First published in Great Britain in 2016 by

MacLehose Press
an imprint of Quercus
Carmelite House
50 Victoria Embankment
London EC4Y 0DZ

An Hachette UK Company

A CIP catalogue record for this book is available
from the British Library.

ISBN (TPB) 978 0 85705 398 5
ISBN (Ebook) 978 0 85705 397 8

10 9 8 7 6 5 4 3 2 1

Designed and typeset in Caslon by Libanus Press, Marlborough
Printed and bound in Great Britain by Clays Ltd, St Ives plc

To Sandro and Dario,
friends and teachers

With a deep distrust and a deeper faith

BEPPE FENOGLIO

I

The door of the hut was ajar. Her body lay in ethereal afternoon light, a pattern of cuts across her bare back, her long black hair spread round her.

He took a couple of hesitant steps, determined to persuade himself nothing had happened, then fell to his knees and stared, hands hanging uselessly by his sides, perhaps no more able to drop his gaze than Hector when he understood Achilles was going to kill him.

2

When the alarm went off Corso was in his sleeping bag, hands behind his head, intently watching his own breath condensing in the cold air, rising to disappear in the darkness.

An hour or maybe two hours before, the distant cry of an animal had woken him, and he had lain motionless, listening, imagining a creature at the point of death or of giving birth, until the cry was lost in the soughing of the wind.

Now he silenced the alarm with a precise gesture of his hand, turned on his torch and checked the Cyma watch on his wrist: 1.57. The wind had dropped and the silence round his tent was full of tiny sounds.

He glanced down at the book he had left open beside his water bottle the night before, its pages turned back and divided unequally, like the wings of a bird forced to fly round in a circle.

He had read that a woman had been telling her husband, just back from a long journey, that while he had been away their little girl had always been quiet and well-behaved, but had eaten almost nothing and had started saying, "don't even think about it," whenever anything was suggested to her. The man sitting on the sofa listened, then took off his shoes and said something that did nothing to solve the problem.

Corso massaged his neck. Two drops of condensation were running down the side of the tent, like translucent insects. Then he pulled trousers and socks from the bottom of his backpack, shoved everything else back into it, and went out.

Outside everything was a uniform grey in the moonlight.

He lit the stove he had left in the shelter of a rock and, while the flame guttered, went down to the lake to fill his small pan and wash his face. On the mirror of water, scarcely larger than the area of a country dance, moon-coloured circles expanded, but by the time he got up to go back to the tent the surface had once more become dark and still.

He dropped a teabag into the little pan and studied the surrounding mountains: ancient peaks a little over three thousand metres, without sudden surges, marked with veins of nickel darkened by water.

He considered why he had come. The evening before, under the setting sun, he had seemed to see beauty in the mountain even if it was a kind of beauty that needs patience to understand. But now she was no more than a triangle of cold shadow.

"Are you really so wicked?" he asked her.

The mountain continued to stare back at him in silence, her profile sharp as the five letters of her name. Corso nodded to show he knew that it would soon be clear, then moved a few steps to one side and opened his trousers to urinate. The night above him was clear, the clouds far off and still. A few stars were visible in the darkest part of the sky.

He took the tent, the bag and the stove out of his backpack, and hid everything under a large stone at the foot of the rock face, gave a last glance at the area of stones he had just crossed and started forward.

He climbed the first few metres slowly, almost indolently, to give his body time to get used to what he was asking of it. The rock, cold but not icy, gave his fingers exactly what it promised, so that his mind slipped quickly into the white room for which he had come: a silent room with no doors hung with a single great picture, and all the time in the world to get to the top of the picture.

He realised he was near the summit when he could see the metal cross damaged years before by a storm. It was hanging head down now, held in place only by a single metal support.

He passed it with a short diagonal walk, and a dozen hand-holds later he was at the summit.

He poured himself some tea from the thermos in his back-pack, and looked down at the area of stones at the foot of the mountain. In the blue moonlight the flint fragments looked like the spines of cold-blooded animals, come over the centuries to die side by side in a cemetery their ancestor had chosen. Beyond that was the perfect opal of the lake, the path, the wood and finally the road, where beside the bridge he could see his own car resting, as small and simple as a tile. Everything seen from up here looked to be motionless but breathing, as it must have been before any life had ever existed.

He passed a hand over his brow, feeling his sweat already caked into a solid dust.

He imagined the last pages of the novel he had been reading: the woman would be in the middle of the room and the man listening to her would be sitting on the sofa with his feet on a low glass table. Behind them would be a light-coloured staircase, as rational and unremarkable as everything else in the house.

He saw himself climbing those stairs and going down a corridor to a room with a partly open door where a little girl of four was asleep, her left leg outside the bedclothes.

He saw himself go in and sit beside her, pushing aside a lock of her fair hair and lightly touching the hollow behind her knee, where blue veins showed through her delicate skin. Then he laid his head on the pillow and stayed with his face very close to her, listening to the soft murmur from her lips, until he became aware of an obscure evil beating in her chest like a second heart.

Then he saw himself get up, go to the window and realise, seeing the headlights of the motionless car below the house, that once out of there he would never be allowed to see the little girl again or know anything about her. Ever again.

Corso leaped to his feet, opening his mouth wide like a drowned man. The darkness round him seemed immense and he felt an urge to jump, until the sight of a lone cloud approaching from the sea, slow and innocent, calmed him. He stopped trembling and mouthing the little girl's name.

To the east, far off across the plain, were shining the bright lights of villages that with a little effort he would have been able to name, and beyond them was the luminous mass of the great city.

He gave these a last glance, before pulling his backpack onto his shoulders and beginning the descent.

The wind had got up and the night was starting to change colour in the east. From far away, on the French side, came the barking of a dog, as if to indicate that something was beginning.

3

He quickly came down the sharply curving mule track, through clumps of alders from which flew out small birds that had spent the night hiding from owls. A few weeks earlier the path had been trodden by cows that had left behind the cold smell of their dung. From somewhere in the darkness echoed the steady sound of a stream.

When he was about a hundred metres from the river he recognised the form of a small off-road vehicle parked next to his Polar. Leaning on the bonnet and looking at him, was a man dressed in grey or blue with a cap on his head. The rifle on his shoulder was softly reflecting the pale moonlight.

He crossed the last few metres without hurrying.

The man waited for him on the parapet of the bridge, staring at the foam under the arch. When Corso approached, he took a packet of cigarettes from the pocket of his jacket and went through the motion of offering it. When Corso shook his head, he raised his face to the moon.

"Are you married?" he said.

He had a dry body and hair as grey as his uniform. Middle-aged.

Corso said no.

"Wise," said the man, puffing smoke from between irregular teeth. "Women cannot understand these places the way we understand them."

He kept the burning end of the cigarette concealed in the hollow of his hand, even though they were not on the bridge of a ship and there was no breath of wind.

"Where have you come down from?"

"The Picca."

"The one over the iron mine?"

"Facing it."

The man took a longer pull on his cigarette.

"My brother's a priest at Comiso. We don't meet very often, but I always ask him why he took the cloth. And he always gives me the same answer: that no-one who hasn't heard the call can ever understand the joy of serving Our Lord." He spat the stub of his cigarette into the river. "So that's why I'm not asking you why you went up there."

Corso made a gesture of agreement that doubled as goodbye and went towards his car. The man came up while he was unlacing his boots and began moving the surrounding grass with his foot as though he had lost something hardly worth looking for.

"There's a dead steinbock under the Picca, did you notice?"

Corso took off his climbing trousers and pulled on his jeans.

"No."

The forester looked towards the valley where the light was getting stronger.

"Two men from Savona shot it and didn't bother to retrieve it. When I confiscated their rifles, one said not to scare him because he had a weak heart." He spat. "Poachers aren't what they used to be. They used to shoot straight at you."

Corso fastened his sandals.

"Have a good day," he said.

As he drove out of the clearing he could see the man lighting another cigarette. He held him in his mirror until the red of the cigarette was swallowed up in the darkness the daylight was not yet strong enough to overcome; then opened the window and stuck out his elbow.

He had seen the steinbock the evening before, when the setting sun had painted yellow the snowfield where the animal was lying. Sitting outside his tent, he had contemplated it at length, but the steinbock never moved, its head turned towards the valley, already one with the substance of stones and bones it had trodden only a few days before. Either a young male or a female, he had thought.

He turned on the car radio and drove for a few kilometres listening to an old song by Françoise Hardy. The words did nothing for him, nor did the tune or even Hardy's face, though he could not get it out of his mind. But he listened to the song right to the end.

When the car came to a group of low buildings, he turned off the radio and slowed down before stopping in front of the last house, distinguished by the yellow sign of a public telephone.

The name of the telephone company had changed twice since the time the sign had been put up. There were no lights in the windows of the house, and but for the sound of Arab music coming from the interior, you would have thought the house had been abandoned for years.

Corso got out of the car, threw a handful of gravel at one of the windows, then turned his back to wait. The house opposite had been done up like a town house, and two demijohns had been left upended to drain under its balcony, along with a motor-cycle and a kennel complete with a steel chain strong enough to tow a steamship.

"Come in," said a dry voice behind him.

Corso climbed three steps to a room with a bar and half a

dozen tables, its walls decorated with the heads of wild boars, steinbocks, chamois and small animals immortalised by the taxidermist in fierce or cunning poses. The floor was covered with tiles decorated with small flowers and beyond a folding partition there was a T.V. set and an antiquated threshing machine.

Corso sat down on one of the stools at the bar.

The tall, thin old man arranging a cup under the spout of the coffee machine looked as if he had just escaped from a hospital, taking advantage of a door left open by mistake, without waiting to comb his white hair or change out of his pyjamas.

"You know someone else who used to be like you?" he said.

Corso was searching for the music he had heard from outside, but the place was silent.

"Nino Oggero." The man answered himself. "An eccentric figure who used to go off alone without saying anything to anyone, until one day he didn't come back. It took us a week to find him. He'd broken his back falling off the Traverso. We never told his mother, but he didn't have a finger nail left, he had struggled so hard trying to get back on his feet."

He put the coffee on the bar.

"He had frozen so fast," here he beat his knuckles on the wooden surface, "that we couldn't even get him off with a shovel. We lit a fire in the hope that might help, but the people who were supposed to be watching the fire at night fell asleep and in the morning there wasn't much left of Nino Oggero's hair. His mother saw him in his coffin with that burnt head, and after that she was good for nothing but church.

Corso took a sip of coffee.

"Didn't his feet get burnt another time?"

The old man studied him carefully, then looked away to the dog stretched out under one of the tables. By now the sky outside had developed a sort of diffused clarity.

17

"What do you think you're looking at?"

The dog lowered guilty eyes.

"If I leave him outside he complains of the cold," the old man shook his head. "And if I keep him inside he complains because it's his nature to be outside. I really ought to take him into the forest with a shovel, and it would be better still if someone else could do the same for me. Hungry?"

"What have you got?"

"There's some boar left."

Corso went into the bathroom, took off his pullover and short-sleeved shirt and washed himself with the piece of soap on the basin. He scratched the dried blood from the wound at the base of his thumb and wrapped it in his handkerchief.

When he came back into the bar he was wearing a clean shirt.

"There was a new forester at the bridge," he said, getting back on the stool.

The frizzling of olive oil could be heard from the kitchen stove. After a while the old man elbowed the curtain aside and placed a plate on the bar containing meat floating in a broth the colour of mercury. Beside this he put a basket of bread.

"Says he caught two poachers from Savona red-handed."

"Naturally," said the old man.

Corso let some fragments of bread fall into his plate.

"Wasn't that what happened?"

"Those two don't even know which end to hold a rifle."

Corso picked up one of the glasses draining on the sink. The old man poured in a finger of tamarind and lengthened it with water, making it the same colour as the shirts of the footballers in the photo propped against the mirror.

"You know why they moved that man here?"

Corso shook his head.

"His brother-in-law controlled some reforestation contracts and found him the job. They were unable to catch him in the act, so they sent him to us."

Corso took a clove out of his mouth and put it on the side of his plate. He'd never liked cloves.

"Where do the two from Savona come in?"

"The fact is," Cesare snorted, "the man must have shot the steinbock himself, but when he found he couldn't retrieve it, he noticed those two horsing about in the forest, and decided to exploit them."

"What d'you mean horsing about . . . ?" Corso began, but seeing the sly smile on Cesare's face, he understood. Although every single one of Cesare's years was marked on his features, his eyes were still alive with the impudence of youth.

He finished what was left on his plate.

"Before you go I want to show you something," Cesare said, realising Corso was about to get up.

They went out the back, where the old man kept some cylinders of gas and an old freezer under a roof. The dog followed, gloomily sniffing at Corso's heels. The light was now strong enough to define shapes but not colours.

The old man opened the freezer and pulled out a package wrapped in nylon and tied with string. Before putting it on the ground and untying it, he called at the dog to keep him away.

"Nice work, don't you think?" he said.

Corso squatted and took a closer look.

"A sheep?"

"A nice big fat one."

Apart from a few shreds of meat, it looked more like a blanket left for several days on a busy road.

"I would not have believed dogs capable of such a thing."

"Dogs aren't."

Corso stared at the old man.

"They're a couple and a boy. Said to be from the Apennines, but I doubt it. A few years ago new people moved into the Mercantour district and I'm sure they've crossed the border from there."

Corso looked at the dismembered animal.

"Has no-one taken a shot at them yet?"

"We can't. We have to keep the carcasses and they'll see if they can reimburse us."

They packed up the carcass again and put it in the freezer. From the corner where he had settled, the dog followed them with his eyes as they went back to the bar. One was opaque, but the other seemed to have inherited its light.

"I'll be off now," Corso said.

The old man pulled out a cloth bag from under the bar.

"Shall I bring you some more?" Corso asked.

"Yes, but short ones where it's hot; you always bring long ones where it's cold."

"How much do I owe you for the food?"

"Let's call it quits with the books."

"I don't make you a present of them."

"I don't want to discuss it."

No sooner was he outside than Corso heard Cesare close the latch behind him. He walked a little way towards his car, then went back and knocked. The door opened immediately.

"When I came I could hear Arab music."

Cesare made as if to put his hand in his pocket, but his pyjamas had no pockets.

"I've got myself a satellite dish," he said.

"To watch Arab television?"

"I like watching plump women dancing in their clothes. Reminds me of old times."

"Just that?"

"No other reason. Now off with you, you've already wasted far too much of my time."

4

When he saw the animal crashing loudly through the thicket, snapping off branches as it came, Jean-Claude Monticelli quickly calculated how much time he would have to enjoy his moment of hunting before it disappeared again into the forest.

He had spent more than three hours waiting for it: it was a male, its back as high as a small boy's shoulder, forelegs strong and slightly curved to drive it forward. Like a cold block of lava hurled horizontally by an explosion.

Hearing the bark of approaching dogs, he decided to fire.

The animal probably noticed a new warmth on its shoulder, nothing to affect its aim or direction.

Jean-Claude Monticelli fired again, and this time a mass of black liquid burst from the neck of the boar, which hesitated, covered another couple of metres, then stopped and went into a ridiculous dance. Then when it saw the dogs emerge from the thicket it gathered itself and lowered its head to get its tusks at the right angle.

The four beaters, noticing the boar was wounded, called off the hounds. They obeyed, except for a couple of young dogs aroused by the smell of blood.

Jean-Claude then let off two shots in quick succession. The first hit the beagle in flight, forcing it to make three turns in the air before hitting the ground almost as if cut in two. The other hit the head of the clay-coloured bloodhound, which collapsed in a more conventional manner.

The boar stood staring at them, then itself fell with the thud of a mattress dropped from a height.

Monticelli approached. It was no bigger than others he had killed but its strength, even now as its life ebbed away, was stretching its skin so tightly as to make it shine. The heat of the chase had made salty designs on its coat, and its penis was erect.

He stooped to touch the wound below the boar's neck from which hot blood was gushing, weakly pumped by the last beats of its heart.

A dozen metres away, the beaters had put their dogs on leads and were talking in a group. One of them was carrying a mongrel over his shoulder: earlier that morning the boar's tusk had pierced its ribs ensuring a clean, rapid death. The two dogs Jean-Claude had fired at were not likely to suffer such a fate.

He got up and beckoned the leader over, running his rifle over the boar's neck to indicate what interested him.

"And five hundred euros for the two dogs," he said.

The man explained in Romanian to the others, who were now smoking, and they nodded their thanks.

5

Corso pulled onto the rough track, and after a couple of corners saw the house perched on the hill like a chevron on a soldier's shoulder. It was a farmhouse like many others, shaped like an L open to the south, with its rooms on the short side, the stable and hayloft on the long side, and a roof like a mirror.

He stopped the car under the roof of an outhouse that would once have been used for agricultural equipment and barrels, and headed for the house. It had the atmosphere of a place where life had called, only to move on elsewhere later. Corso had been living there for fifteen years. When he moved in he had limited himself to checking the roof, whitewashing a couple of rooms and shutting off unused areas to keep animals out. Otherwise it was just as his mother had left it a quarter of a century before, with marks of damp on its cream-coloured façade, unreliable gutters and drainpipes and the slow insinuation of grass into the brick paving.

As he crossed the yard he noticed the marks made in the dust by the postman's motor scooter. This was an unusual spring: dry, firm and soporific like summer. Only the vines seemed to appreciate the drought.

Passing the postbox, he ran up the stairs two at a time and went in. He was welcomed by the fresh smell of saltpetre. Putting his backpack and the bag of books returned by Cesare down by the only armchair, he went over to the sink for a glass of water, then headed for the bedroom.

Here he pulled a leather bag from the wardrobe, and took out of it a case, several plastic covers and a pair of rubber gloves that he pulled on before going back through the kitchen.

The sound of his key in the postbox echoed through the yard. He looked at the red stamp on the envelope with its typewritten address, then took the letter back with him into the house.

Sitting at the table, he opened the envelope with the paper knife he had taken from the case and read the two lines in the centre of the page. These had been written with a pen, in a free but sober script. Putting the paper back into the envelope, he sealed it in one of the transparent plastic covers he had prepared.

As he was putting it away, he heard the barking of the dog kept by its owners to guard the vegetable gardens on the hill.

Looking out of the window facing the back, Corso could see his uncle and Elio crossing what was left of the vineyard like two elderly partisans, still wearing the same clothes as when they had left home. His uncle was in rubber leggings and the grey overalls of a mechanic, while Elio, in hunting jacket and khaki trousers, looked more like an English officer just landed by parachute. His thick hair was dazzling white against the dusty green vegetation.

By the time Corso left the house the two were already in the yard.

"It's criminal to let a vineyard go to ruin like that," Elio said.

Corso glanced briefly at the hillside where posts from the old trellis could just be made out among the thorns, then shook the hand Elio held out to him and exchanged nods with his uncle.

"How's your son?"

Elio said that apart from the danger of exploding mines

things were fine, then gave a smile in no way related to what he had just said, and turned back to look towards the vineyard again.

Elio, a dozen years older than Corso and a dozen years younger than Corso's uncle, was a widower who owned a wine-producing firm. He had a son who was a professional soldier stationed in Afghanistan, and a daughter married in Luxembourg who came back at Easter and for the grape harvest.

When his wife died eight years ago, Elio had suffered from a form of depression that took away his taste for food and work. His daughter had taken him with her and had him treated by a Vietnamese acupuncturist. The only thing anyone who didn't know him could have said of him was that he was a strong-willed man at peace with himself, and with an unusually full head of hair for his age.

"Elio has come with me because he has something to say," Corso's uncle said.

Elio was still staring at the hillside.

"Come in and let's sit down for a bit, then."

Back inside, Corso prepared the percolator and put it to heat. Elio and the uncle sat down at the table. Except for the refrigerator, cooking stove, heater, armchair and sink, there was nothing large in the room, nor for that matter anything small: no ashtrays or pictures on the walls. Neither were there any curtains, and the floor was rough bare brick.

"Lots of men of my age – and even older – go to a nightclub or casino every week," Elio said. "They spend their money there and go home again happy, and good for them. But I'm not like that. If I'm not in the vineyard by six, and don't spend the evening in the cellars, I feel I've wasted the whole day. That's just the way I'm made. Each to his own."

He looked at Corso, then went back to watching his fingers

tapping a pattern on the waxed cloth as he struggled to shape what he was trying to say.

"But eventually," he went on, "you realise if you don't share your pleasures they'll end up turning bitter. So I've told myself that since the good Lord has decided Caterina cannot enjoy the family inheritance, maybe I should share it with someone else."

The bubbling of the coffee slowly got louder. Corso took the percolator off the stove, poured the coffee into little cups and put sugar on the table. Each man took a single spoonful.

"Who is the lady?" Corso said.

Elio looked first at the uncle, then at Corso.

"The Romanian who works at the bar."

Corso held his cup suspended for a moment, then drank.

"She has faith," he said, cradling his cup in the palm of his hand. "Like a small bird with no nest."

Elio agreed. "Her husband has disappeared with the money she was sending home so they could build a house. No-one knows what's happened to him, but he's not likely to be seen again. The wife of one of my workers who comes from the same village told me that. Meanwhile the children are with their grandmother, but their mother would like to bring them to Italy."

"Have you ever spoken to her yourself?"

Elio shrugged.

"Just a few words when she came for the harvest. I got the impression of a woman who doesn't waste time chasing after butterflies. I know that after she finishes work in the bar she goes to clean school gymnasiums. As far as I'm concerned, I'd be willing to take her into my house and make it possible for her children to study up to whatever level they like. She can come and work in the firm or stay at the bar, whichever she prefers, and when her papers are in order I'd be ready to settle her properly. I shall leave the firm to Cristina and Davide, but she and her children will never want for anything."

Corso took his cup to the sink and went to lean against the side of the window. Beyond the road there were no vineyards but fields, with only a few trees to mark boundaries. On the far side of the yard, in a corner of the roofed area, two abandoned tractors sat side by side like a mother and son who have nothing in common.

"People don't work through agents these days," Corso said. "It'll look better if you go and talk to her yourself."

For a long time the room was full of whatever silence is possible between three naturally taciturn men who have a lot to say, then Elio pushed his chair back.

"Where's your bathroom?" he said. "I'd like to use it a moment if you don't mind."

Corso indicated the door, then went back to the window. Three children were pedalling mountain bikes in single file along the main road. As soon as water could be heard running into the basin on the other side of the wall, Corso's uncle shifted his weight, causing his chair to squeak.

"When we went to get your father at Mango," he said, "the reds were only waiting for an order from their commanders to put him up against the wall. There were five of us: Graglia's father, the two Oggeros, Elio's older brother and me. It was only three days after the end of the war and not many people were ready to kick the bucket in order to save someone who'd been firing at them only a week before, but Elio's brother was the first to climb on the chest behind the Breda machine gun. He knew if things went wrong the reds would let loose the first shots against whoever was behind the Breda, but he put himself there all the same." Corso's uncle paused to shift the Toscano cigar in his mouth. "It would be a good thing for the woman.

They have a habit in that family for doing what is right and proper."

The bathroom door opened. Corso heard Elio crossing the room and sitting down again. The rearmost of the children had fallen off his bike and was watching the other two disappear without looking back.

"I know it's not usual," Elio said, "but I'm sure if you do go and talk to her we'll be able to fix things."

Corso went on looking at the road where the little boy, now back in the saddle, was pedalling savagely towards the village using only one leg.

6

Last time he had seen the station it had been swathed in great expanses of white cloth, and the route to the exit defined by a labyrinth of drapery. Now, unmasked, Porta Nuova was all plasterboard, artificial lighting, a bookshop, bar, clothes shops, Japanese food, a supermarket and the same famous brands as can be seen in the station of every other great city. All that was left of the old, bare, grandiloquent Savoyard entrance hall was its lofty ceiling, lit by great windows, through which came the rumble and roar of the eternally sleepy traffic outside on Corso Vittorio.

He took a tram, getting out on the shady side of a round, sunny square.

With his hands in his pockets and sleeves rolled up to the elbow, he contemplated the monument, the suspended wires that surrounded it, and the benches where he had sat as student, husband and then as a father.

He had loved this city from the first day he had set foot in it until the night when, on one of those very benches, he had tried to think of the most practical way to escape from it. Between that day and that night, almost his whole life had passed, or at least what mattered of it.

Crossing the road, he entered a cul-de-sac leading up to a solid brick building, and climbed the steps to the eighteenth-century entrance hall on the first floor, now defiled by a crude display of regulations and circulars. Inside a Plexiglas booth, a young man in uniform who resembled a prehistoric bird looked up from his monitor.

"Yes?"

Corso was about to speak when a fit of coughing made them both turn towards a door from where, leaning against the jamb, a short dark man was staring at them.

"Well?"

Corso nodded. The man had another fit of coughing before signing to him to follow. They went down the corridor, the man balancing his low centre of gravity on short stumpy legs, as graceless as a machine created for hard work. Corso followed two paces behind: tall, with the legs of a horse and shoulders broad enough to sustain the slightly curved musculature of his back.

As they passed, one of the old guard might look up from a pile of papers behind the American-style windows of the offices. Or touch a youngster on the shoulder as if to say, "Just look who it is," but always in silence, as if at the passage of a procession beginning or ending in disaster.

"Commissario Bramard." A little man as slight as a house of cards leaned out into the corridor. "Still on top form?"

"That'll do, Pedrelli, that'll do." Corso squeezed the man's hand as he passed without slowing down.

Before entering the door marked COMMISSARIO ARCADI-PANE, Corso noticed a girl dressed in black, one side of her skull shaved bald and with a small spoon through the lobe of one ear. She was sitting in a cubicle with a grizzled policeman, and looked very much as if she were about to drown in a sea of troubles. It was only a momentary thought, then Corso went through the door.

In the office a heavy weight of heat and smoke weighed on the seventies furnishings. "Air conditioning out of order," Arcadipane said. "Sit down and don't mention it."

The two sides of the room not occupied by shelves or the window contained a sofa that looked as if someone had left a boiling pan on it, and a grey door, which led nowhere, as Corso knew.

He sat down on one of the two chairs facing the desk.

Arcadipane pulled down the blind to shield their eyes from the sun, opened the window a little, then sat down in his comfortable armchair in the manner you would expect from a man of forty-three with a strong south Italian accent, a monthly salary of 2,400 euros, and a great many worries.

"What gets on my tits," he began, passing a hand through the few hairs that still survived at the back of his skull, "is that your hair isn't falling out. What do you do? Wash it with the yolks of eggs from your hens?"

Corso pushed away the ashtray overflowing with fag-ends before him. Everything in the room stank of cheap tobacco and deodorant used to mask the smell of cheap tobacco.

"How's your family?" he asked.

"Mariangela had a growth on her breast," Arcadipane said briefly, "but that was no problem. The girl's having her first period and Luca may be put back a year at school, though he's beginning to train with the first team. You still teaching?"

"Yes."

"Still part-time?"

"O.K., that brings us up to date. Now let's get to the point."

Corso took the plastic envelope from his pocket and held it out to Arcadipane.

"Where did that come from?" Arcadipane said, studying the stamp on the envelope.

"Romania."

"And inside?"

"Written in English. *And mercy on our uniform, man of peace or man of war: the peacock spreads his fan.*"

"What does that mean?"

"It's the final words of a song."

Arcadipane weighed the letter in his hand, then let it fall on the desk and took some cigarettes from the top drawer of his desk. Despite his jacket and carefully trimmed moustache, no-one could have mistaken him for a French pianist: his face was directly descended from ancestors with coarse faces, curved legs and complexions that opposition instantly clouded. His mind was sharp, which was why for ten years now he had been sitting on that side of the desk, why Corso had not been worried to see him take over, and also why he was there again now.

"How many letters counting this one?" said the commissario, lighting his Muratti cigarette with a Pope Pius lighter, which he then dropped back into his pocket.

"Thirteen, all from different countries," Corso said, leaning back in his chair to avoid the first puff of smoke. "The shortest time between one and the next has been five months, the longest a year and seven months. The address on the envelope is always typed on the same 1972 Olivetti, and the words of the song are always handwritten with the same Montblanc pen. No finger-prints or traces of D.N.A. The calligraphic features indicate a man: confidence, self-control, perfectionism. Controlled emotions, ready intelligence, conspicuous narcissism, compulsive correct-ness and a complete absence of emotive empathy."

Arcadipane balanced the ashtray on top of a pile of folders marked with the rubber stamp of the police.

"Could be yourself?" he suggested. Along the edge of the desk were several mugshot photographs and a wrapper held together by three rubber bands. He pulled twice more on his cigarette in a meditative manner.

"Perhaps now twenty years have passed we could consider the hypothesis that Autumnal might be more than one person, don't you think? Passing themselves off as a sort of witness."

"We could, but that's not the case."

Arcadipane locked his hands behind his head and contemplated the opaque spherical lampshade. City noises, including the distinctive sound of a tram followed by a hooter, came in through the window. And from beyond the door, telephones and voices.

"So this is the moment when you think I ought to bury the whole thing under a stone?" Corso said.

Arcadipane looked askance at him, but did not move.

"You know the odds against catching a murderer after . . ."

"Seven months ago it was 0.3 per cent. Is it worse now?"

The commissario smoked without narrowing his eyes.

"You were the best. And you couldn't do it."

"The best find people alive and catch those responsible. The worst only find dead bodies, and maybe not even that."

Arcadipane held Corso's gaze, then looked back at the ceiling. Someone was walking on the floor above. A woman's heels. The sound moved away. Then from the street below came men's voices, quarrelling about right of way.

"You know who we've had under house arrest since last week?" Arcadipane said, as though talking to the cloud of smoke suspended under the ceiling.

"Morabito."

"So you do read the papers!"

"I heard it on the radio."

Arcadipane reached for a folder fastened by a single green rubber band and pulled it towards himself. In doing so he

34

knocked against the ashtray and tipped a mound of grey onto the desk.

"Our friend Morabito Antonio . . ." he read from the folder, ignoring the spilt ash, ". . . five prostitutes killed between '81 and September '83. All stabbed in the belly. Never fewer than ten wounds: a generous man. Repressed sexuality, erectile problems, hatred of women, the whole caboodle. If not caught he would undoubtedly have killed again . . ." He ran his eyes down the page. "A round twenty-five years . . . No mental problems. In prison he had behaved perfectly, studied for a degree and collaborated with the internet site of a centre for long-distance adoptions."

"A degree in what?"

Arcadipane turned a couple of pages.

"Psychology." He stubbed out his fag-end. "What do you think about that?"

Corso scratched a drop of resin off his trousers. The pines. The mountain. The climb.

"You know what a psychologist would say? Perhaps even Morabito?"

"I know I'm about to find out."

"He'd say I'm the last person you should ask for advice, given that my vision of reality is strongly compromised by self-harm, guilt, the failure to grieve, and a dozen other problems that make me a borderline case. Not to speak of the difficulty of controlling feelings already dominant in me before it happened."

"I've been taking notes. What would you do?"

Corso stared at the light mark that the resin had left on the worn fabric of his trousers.

"I'd put a man on it for a month and keep an eye on his computer and the sites he visits. If he goes back to prostitutes and violent porn, I'd have a few relevant things to say."

"But it's not certain he'd start again, surely?"

Corso got up and went to the door.

"You'll call me when you get the report from the lab?"

Arcadipane looked up at the ceiling.

"Close the door on your way out so I don't lose all this nice fresh air."

7

The train crossed monotonous fields of maize which a few more weeks would turn a beautiful golden colour, then skirted the foundry before slowing down near the corrugated iron of the nomads' camp and coming to rest in the station, under the shadow of the large and newly repainted silos.

Corso came out by the underpass, with labourers and other workers on their way home. The town was neither big nor small, not entirely agricultural and no longer industrial, not traditional and yet unchanging.

He crossed what passed for a square, with its bar, its ugly monument to the Alpine troops and its circular pool full of fish with unhealthy white excrescences, on the way to the car park. When the soil began to turn red and the houses gave way to farmhouses, he stopped at a trattoria for lorry drivers, where he helped himself from a table of antipasti and ordered a marinated steak. The place had a public payphone. He dialled a number but there was no answer. Going back to his table, he ate the steak the waitress had left for him, paid and left.

It was just after nine when he reached Santo Stefano; the air was clear and the moon so bright that the outlines of the distant fortresses that had once protected the road to the sea were clearly visible.

Leaving the main road, he followed a rough track furrowed

by tractor wheels until he reached a small grass clearing from which the hill began to fall away. He could hear a few dogs barking on the farms, but when he came to the back of the house all was silent.

He whistled up to a window on the second floor, where the moving light from a T.V. could be seen.

There was light in the apartment below, but no sign of the old woman or her carer who lived there. It was said locally that the woman kept hidden in her house a box of Marengo gold coins inherited from her grandfather who had been tax collector for the king, and that the carer had originally been her husband's mistress, staying on with the widow in the hope of sooner or later finding where she had hidden the gold. The two women, united in their terror of burglars, would keep the light on all night.

After waiting longer than seemed necessary, Corso walked round the house and rang the bell.

"Corso," he said into the intercom.

When he reached the landing, Elena's face appeared in the half-open door.

"Wednesdays I have to clean the school gym," she said

Corso looked at the fair hair tucked behind her beautifully chiselled left ear.

"I know. I tried to phone."

"I was in the shower."

"I only need five minutes."

On the kitchen table were a dirty dish, a fork and a glass with a little wine at the bottom, and the remains of an apple. Elena sat down. Her eyes were warm and dark, the colour of newly turned earth. She had on a blue vest and tracksuit trousers. Her feet were bare.

"Someone has asked me to make you an offer," Corso said, still standing.

The room was fitted out with second-hand furniture. The fridge, designed to form part of a kitchen suite, stood alone. The T.V. was murmuring quietly in the corner.

"Who?"

"Elio Gallo."

"That rich guy who makes wine?"

"He's ready to arrange for your children to come to Italy for their education, and as soon as you've sorted things out with your husband he'd be happy to marry you."

Elena looked steadily at him.

"Why have you come to tell me this?"

She was thin and her eyes were those of a woman vulnerable to uncertainty. Corso loved her.

"I owe him," he said.

"Money?"

"Not money."

"What then?"

"No matter. I promised him I would tell you and I've done it. You're free to say yes or no."

Elena got up, gathered the dishes together and took everything to the sink. The skin above the neckline of her vest was the colour of ivory.

"Don't you owe something to me too?" she said turning on the water as if to rinse the washing-up.

"What I owe you is honesty and . . . and I have been honest."

She made a gesture as if to free her face of something that annoyed her, then smiled.

"When I came back, Adrian took me to see the building. He told me our apartment would be on the top floor. A fine view. And near the school for the children. He was being honest then, too."

Corso took a couple of steps towards the sink, picked up the glass she had used, filled it and drank. Their shoulders were very close.

"Elio's a good man," he said. "When he says he'll do something, he does it. And I'm doing the same thing now."

They went down one behind the other, their feet meeting the stairs in unison. In front of the outer door they stopped in the circle of light from the single lamp lighting the road. Elena zipped up her jacket, and took her helmet in one hand and the bag with the white coat she wore for work in the other. Her face, in the weak light, was magnificent in its pallor.

"I need a month to think," she said.

Corso nodded. The clock struck some nocturnal hour.

"I had an uncle like you," she smiled. "Few people came to his funeral and none of them knew who the others were. They all kept silent because they were all afraid of finding out they'd come to the wrong church."

By the time he heard Elena's old Ciao bicycle move off, Corso was already climbing back up the hill. He stopped to watch her lamp until it was swallowed up by the first houses of the village. A few minutes later he saw the lights come on in the gym.

He turned back and continued climbing.

The surrounding hills were like ashes under the indifferent moon.

8

Opening the door of the room, Jean-Claude Monticelli found the girl sitting cross-legged on the bed watching television.

She looked as if she could have been the younger sister of the girl on the first evening: the same fair hair, small high breasts, girlish legs, cheap shoes, leggings and sleeveless shirt with spangles. But this girl was wearing lighter make-up and had a less experienced look.

Jean-Claude closed the door and let the oilskin he had put on when it started raining in the forest slide to the floor. A paradoxical rain, fine and cold, with the sun reddening the unclouded part of the sky. What a pity, he thought, when he had almost reached the cars, not to be alone.

The girl took her feet off the bed, smiled and made a gesture as if to say, "Did you win?"

Jean-Claude spoke to her in English. It took only a few seconds. She took the money and left. There were no unstated questions in her eyes. It must often happen that men came back tired from hunting, thinking yes but then deciding no for various reasons, sometimes bizarre ones like faithfulness, fear of failure or of falling in love: matters of small interest to her and that did not concern him in the least.

He took a shower, made a call to Switzerland from his room

and settled a couple of work problems with a yes and a no, then went down to dinner.

Each of the sixteen tables in the dining room had been set for two. He was shown to one near the fireplace, and the second setting was taken away. While waiting for his venison and vegetables he drank half a bottle of the French red wine he had ordered.

The men in the room were mostly businessmen sitting with young women who were leaning towards them as though what they had to say must contain fascinating new information about the Holy Grail or the assassination of President Kennedy. But in fact the men were talking in various languages about contracts they had signed during the day, or not been able to sign because of bureaucracy or corruption in the country where they were dining and where, for the right payment, they would that night be able to make love.

Jean-Claude ate his venison and went out to smoke on the terrace. At the far end of the loggia, leaning on the balustrade, was a man several years older than himself whose business was trading in the sperm of bulls. Three days before they had exchanged a few words, but now each smoked his cigar facing a different part of the city.

A waiter approached: there was a telephone call for him.

Monticelli went to one of the mahogany and red velvet kiosks facing reception. He lifted the receiver and listened.

"The address?" he said, when the other speaker paused.

"I hope he's there," he said, replacing the receiver.

Leaving the kiosk, he went to the bar. Many of the men had moved there from the restaurant. They were drinking whisky, cognac or Italian liqueurs. Their girls, who had ordered colourful cocktails, were beginning to look tired, wearing fixed smiles.

Monticelli leaned back against the baluster and relit his cigar.

He thought he recognised the girl from his room at one of the tables, or it could have been her sister, but the first mouthful of cigar smoke banished the notion.

He looked towards the door leading to the terrace.

It was a calm night, and there was no noise from the park round the hotel. The surrounding wall and the security reassured him. Good to know that beyond that wall was a city heavy with smells, instincts and impunity.

9

Sitting on the steps in front of the school entrance, Corso watched the five students who had just appeared beyond the fence. They were standing in a circle smoking in silence, and every so often they would look at the building behind them, its façade hung with the Italian flag, the flag of the region and the blue flag of the European Community. The lights were on in the entrance hall, but inside no-one was moving. The only noise was that of heavy lorries on the nearby ring road.

Corso took a sucai lozenge from his pocket and put it in his mouth.

He did not know the names of the five, but knew that they came from a village on the border of the next province, a sprawling community where they grew leeks and had a large arena for Italian-style bowls that could accommodate five hundred spectators under cover. Also, that they came on the bus used by the foundry workers, which was why they were always the first to arrive.

Now two coaches, one blue and the other orange, came into the avenue.

Corso closed his eyes to enjoy the last tiny sounds in the morning air without interruption. Then he opened them again to watch a river of jeans, knapsacks and bomber jackets pour out of the buses.

The males, no sooner off the bus, would go to lean against the railings, light cigarettes and pretend either to talk among themselves or be entirely solitary, as they supervised the coming and going of the girls who ran backwards and forwards to hug their female friends, cut their female enemies and rattle on about the countless things they needed urgently to say. A few newly established couples kissed and scrutinised each other minutely at close quarters. More familiar couples went to sit on the low wall on the other side of the road. At the far end of the gardens a dawdling crowd from the train station now appeared, among them a teacher walking alone with bowed head like a priest on a carnival float.

"Are you going to honour us with your presence at work today?"

Corso turned. A young woman was smiling at him from the door, long brown hair swept over one shoulder and lots of freckles on her neat nose. Behind her a caretaker in blue overalls was crossing the hall carrying two small cups of coffee.

"Oh dear, you've caught me out." Corso got to his feet. "I can't pretend to be off sick any longer."

They climbed the stairs to the second floor. The staffroom was deserted, though still permeated by the smells of the previous day. On the lockers, together with the teachers' names printed in relief on blue plastic labels, old stickers could still be seen: a Madonna with a goldfinch, the tongue of a Rolling Stone, a Smurf saying I HATE STUDENTS, and a trade union logo that didn't quite manage to conceal the word SHITHEAD – relics of a sit-in.

The first bell sounded. Two colleagues came into the room, discussing Puccini's "La Fanciulla del West" which they had seen the previous evening with Friends of Opera, and complaining about the lack of punctuality of the coach.

45

Corso took off the velvet jacket with patched elbows that he kept for school; he wore his windcheater on all other occasions.

As a student he had had a black leather jacket, and as a policeman an inside-out sheepskin. He had almost forgotten his short period in uniform, apart from the poor-quality shoelaces and the marks the cap left on his forehead.

Moving to the window, he watched the students beginning to pile into the building, behind them the ancient communal tower, the grey rectangle of the farmers' union and the curtain of blocks of flats beyond which the silos near the station could be glimpsed.

"A pretty sight, don't you think?"

Corso lowered his eyes as far as the windows of the primary school opposite, where the small children invading the class-rooms were coagulating in groups of three or four according to mysterious laws presumably related in some way to electricity and metals.

"Sleeping bag?" Monica picked a feather from his hair.

"Yes."

"In the mountains?"

"Yes."

"Coffee?"

"Good idea."

They walked carefully so as not to be swept along by the students. As they reached the machine the second bell sounded. Monica pushed in two coins and it began pouring something beige into a cup.

"There's a problem with the Lafleur girl and the swimming course."

"What sort of problem?"

"Shall I give you the long version or the brutal version?"

"As you like."

46

"O.K., she's a bit hairy, sort of round the groin, and the others tease her."

Corso took the cup Monica was holding out to him.

"What about her parents?"

"I've talked to them, but they don't want the hair removed."

"Why not?"

Monica thought for a minute, noticing Corso's injured thumb.

"Promise not to laugh?"

"I promise."

"They're afraid it might make her too appetising."

Three girls with bare midriffs passed. Two of them had braces on their teeth and the third was Chinese. Corso inserted another coin for a second coffee. The caretaker hobbled past with the sad look of a cabaret singer.

"Well? Have you nothing to say?" Monica pressed him.

"You're her support teacher."

"Yes, but when they kept her out of school it was you who went to the camp to persuade them not to."

"They tried to sell me a watch."

"Just their way of being friendly."

"And a moped."

"I thought you liked gypsies."

"And what else?"

"They said you were a bear, but progressive."

Two colleagues came up to them. The man was young, taught mathematics and wore a waistcoat with a diamond pattern; though bald, he still had a strip of hair round his neck like a shredded headrest. Another few weeks, and the woman he was talking to would be retiring after thirty years on the staff. Her colleagues had organised a party for her in the lab, and given her a present which revealed how little they knew about her.

But she had thanked them sincerely all the same.

The caretaker hobbled up.

"Professore Bramard? A phone call for you."

Corso swallowed his last drop of coffee and threw the cup into the bin.

"You'll think about the Lafleur problem, won't you?"

"Ridiculous though it may seem, might the girl's parents not be right?"

"Yes."

"Well, there you are."

The telephone was next to an alcove where two female caretakers spent the morning reading a magazine called *True Stories*. The receiver was lying on the desk.

"Bramard," Corso said.

"It's me."

"Well?"

"There was a hair in that envelope."

Corso said nothing. The third and final bell sounded. The classrooms began to suck back the unwilling students.

"How long will it take to find out more?"

"A day or two. Depends on how much they need to do down at the lab."

A boy looked out of a classroom at the far end of the corridor. Corso raised his hand to show he would be with them in a moment.

The boy nodded, and vanished to give the disappointing news to his classmates.

IO

For the next three days it rained, then the sun returned, then it rained again.

Corso met the second downpour on the hillside, while climbing down a steep slope. Like a horse facing a storm, he stopped motionless to wait while the worst passed, then realising the deluge would continue for some time, he rounded a corner to continue his descent in such a way as to keep the rain out of his face.

At Cesare's bar, a group of young people who had decided not to climb that morning because of the bad weather, were drinking in a corner. They had already got through a good number of beers and were loudly exchanging confidences. The regulars, occupying two tables and only interested in playing cards, took no notice, the gentian liqueur in their glasses merely slowing down the day for them.

Corso handed Cesare his bag of books, then headed for the bathroom to change out of his sodden clothes. The sucai lozenge in his mouth had turned to a granular mush and he threw it down the toilet. He came back to find his tamarind waiting for him on the bar.

He spent half an hour there drying out while Cesare, behind the bar, poured beer, gentian and cognac. No table service. Neither said anything. No mention of foresters or wolves or

49

Arab music: it was understood between them that few subjects were worth extended conversation. When one of the mountaineers, coming to the bar to order another round of drinks, asked Corso if he had just come back from a climb, Corso said no.

"Be careful not to make any friends," muttered Cesare, using up a large part of his own share of words.

When he got home, Corso corrected homework in the cool of the kitchen, repaired a chair, prepared a history lesson on the Spanish Civil War and read three stories by Maupassant. The second of these reminded him of one of his first cases. It involved a prostitute (though he would never have called her that at the time), her pimp and an old man who had worked as a chef on cruise liners. The one who came off worst had been the pimp. That case had been Corso's baptism of truth. It was then that he had realised that working this out had been more than anything a great sorrow: the old man and the prostitute in the story were decent people, full of feeling and with no great criminal intelligence, while the pimp was a scoundrel. The temptation to pretend not to have understood what he could not help understanding came to him that evening, and after a night spent thinking about the matter, he had concluded that he was now at a parting of the ways, whether to be a policeman or something else. So next morning he had the people involved taken to the police station and helped the police uncover the facts. It had needed lots of coffee, far too many cigarettes and a good dose of silence, but these had not cost him too much. Ever after he had avoided such nights: after all, better to avoid unnecessary pain by going straight to the truth. Then tidy the whole thing up, pass it on to someone who knew what to do with it, and go off for a walk. The other thing he had learnt on that occasion was that six cases out of ten can be solved through something known by a prostitute.

In the evening he made himself two eggs which he ate with some week-old rye bread as he watched the sun setting through the window: a modest, well-balanced sunset. Then he washed the dishes, filled his trouser pockets with handfuls of sucai lozenges and put out the light.

As had happened more than once recently he slept a couple of hours, woke under the impression he had heard the telephone ring, then continued to stare in the feeble light from the window, seeing again Michelle's hair spread out on the floor and the cuts on her naked back.

Time had blurred many things but not that image. And he knew why.

The mechanism is always the same: something penetrates us from outside, reverberating in an entirely unexpected way, and showing us we are not as we thought we were. Sometimes the adjustment may only be small, at other times a complete change of direction, but in all cases the image we had of ourselves is shown to have been incomplete if not completely false, and we ourselves are shown to have been more deficient and fragile and immersed in darkness than we had realised. This is the real cutting of the umbilical cord in every life, before which we imagine ourselves to be someone we then realise we can never be again. The moment when innocence ends.

Contrary to what everyone thought, it was not the death of Michelle, the fruitless search for Martina, the loneliness, the loss of his job and finally his taking to drink, that had made him into the man he was now. The cutting of the umbilical cord always coincides with a specific moment, a sharp precise knock that forces one's life to change direction. In his case that moment had been when, with the door of the hut ajar, he had become aware of beauty, where the man he thought he was would only have recognised horror. That had been his umbilical moment, the point of fundamental change in his life that saved that moment from oblivion, just as a drop of amber can fix for all eternity the insect that happens to be caught inside it.

At three in the morning, or it may have been four, he went down to the cellar where the barrels had once been kept and where now the walls were lined to the ceiling with old shelves full of books.

Going to the furthest wall, he emptied some of the shelves of books and removed them. There was a low door in the wall. He pushed it open and switched on the light behind it.

The space, narrow and windowless, contained only large cardboard boxes. He lifted one down; it was damaged and grey with dust, its corners nibbled by mice.

He opened it: old L.P. records; he closed it again.

The second box contained kitchen equipment: whisks, wooden spoons, scales and the blender he had used to mix Martina's first paps and the flans Michelle had loved so much; vegetable purée, gazpacho and sauces for boiled meat. He had been a good cook, perhaps he had even been a good person; he and Michelle had cooked together, and been good together.

In one of the lower boxes were little shoes, bonnets crocheted for the baby by Michelle's mother in Lyons and little gloves. Wonderful things, but frightening now.

He sniffed a yellow romper suit: it smelled only of mould. Infancy, milk, shit and vomit had all vanished. Things needed to preserve existing life and generate new life. A mechanism that in his case had failed.

It took him half an hour to find what he was looking for.

When he had it in his hands he sat down and opened a folder marked AUTUMNAL.

Inside in a plastic cover were photos of the women, and close-ups of the cuts on their backs, their feet, slashed throats and hair, always black, cut off and strewn about. Also the technical reports and useless transcripts of evidence from relatives, dates, times and plans of the huts where the victims had been found, with pictures of objects found at the scene of the crime, and photocopies of the letters that had indicated where to find them, all typed on a 1972 Olivetti. Then his own notebooks, written up in a tiny script exuding logic and confidence with drawings, plans, tables and literary quotations, but in fact no more than monuments to his presumption and failure.

He took the folder out into the courtyard.

An amazing wind, almost a summer wind, was bending the tops of the trees as if in a circular motion. In fact, two winds were meeting: one from the sea, the other from the mountains, with the colder one winning.

Once he had been not only a husband, a father, a good cook and a man who believed in more than one thing; he had also been a smoker. He had not lit a cigarette for eighteen years, but now he would happily have done so, because he felt that in one way or another the matter might end here.

II

The young salesman was occupied with a couple of customers aged about forty, not tall, one wearing a buckskin jacket and the other a leather sports jacket and expensive shoes of military appearance.

Possibly brothers, they were circulating lazily among high-powered B.M.W.s, Audis and Mercedes, opening their bonnets and leaning down to examine the treads of tyres, as if checking the genitals of a bull at a country fair.

The salesman did not bother them. He knew where most of his clients had come from and how they had procured the ticket that had enabled them to climb out of the shit into which they had been born. Besides, despite his youth, he was more intelligent than they were and felt no need to show it. Their money attracted him up to a point, but he was more interested in holding the reins than in driving the cart and its contents home.

A patient predator, thought Jean-Claude Monticelli, who had been watching him for some time.

"Please take a seat," the woman at reception had said in English with a smile when he came in. She lifted her telephone to speak a single word into it, then went back to work on her computer. She was about fifty, sinuous, perfectly at ease in her low-cut blouse.

Without taking off his coat – on which a few flakes of spring snow were melting – Monticelli settled into one of three arm-chairs. The room smelt pleasantly of menthol, and watching the salesman and his two clients in the showroom through the glass would serve to pass the time.

The woman spoke again: "Could you follow me, please?"

Monticelli picked up his overnight case, gave a last glance at the salesman, and followed the woman.

Crossing the workshop, they came out into a courtyard where the snow had melted. The sky was now producing a sort of un-certain sleet, which the woman merely acknowledged by raising her eyes without covering her head. Despite her slim figure and many other notable features, she had the melancholy air often found in women who were exceptionally beautiful when young. You can see the same thing in the eyes of tennis champions who have retired prematurely, Jean-Claude thought.

The woman knocked on the door of a container, excused herself politely and went back to her office.

Entering, Monticelli noticed the extreme softness of moqu-ette carpet under his feet. He walked towards the metal table at the centre of this unusual office. Its sides were lined with wall-paper with a wavy pattern and a few posters of cars. The face of the man behind the desk still retained something of the boy he must have been a dozen years earlier.

"Adrian?" Monticelli asked.

The boy-man smiled and indicated he should take a seat. Monticelli stayed standing and looked at the gold chain on the man's hairless chest, at the breastbone emerging from the neck of his red shirt, and at the little rudder on the chain round his neck. The man's teeth were a masterpiece.

"You are Adrian?" he repeated.

The boy-man again pointed to the chair with one hand and

with the other opened the folder lying before him on the desk. Monticelli glanced briefly at the photos but did not move. A large vehicle of some kind passed outside, making the floor shake.

"Adrian has a problem," the boy-man said, realising the man standing before him would not sit until he had an answer. "Just as I do."

Monticelli nodded his understanding, turned and left.

As he crossed the courtyard he heard the boy-man call out behind him, then curse.

In the office the two brothers were signing papers, supervised by the woman. The salesman, standing aside, was drinking coffee. Outside the sleet had given way to an all-enveloping sunlight. God, how the weather keeps changing, Monticelli thought, raising his face to enjoy the unexpected warmth.

12

"Is the seven already down?"

"I didn't come here to talk."

"But like this you're handing it on a plate to Corso."

"Should I pocket it then?"

"If you'd played it instead of matching that pair, we'd have been home and dry by now."

"Are we supposed to be talking or playing? If talking, I'd rather have stayed at home with Rita."

Elena appeared in the room, just long enough to attract his attention with a wave of the hand. Corso threw down the seven, passed the cards won to his partner to count, and got to his feet. Pushing aside the two lamps once used to light the billiard table, he crossed the room. On the long wall were the blackboard and the rack for cues, relics of the billiards. Everyone knew the story: a dozen years before, at the same time as money for the wine, travelling salesmen had appeared in the district with cars full of samples, vacuum cleaners and computer catalogues. At lunch-time they stopped at the bar for a bite and a chat ("We've just been allotted this area"), and after emptying a glass and asking for some information, they had suggested a game, just to pass the time till their customer opened his shop. The first few times they lost or at least did not win. After a few days they were back for another game and someone, it may have been one of them, suggested playing for money. Eventually they hit on the right person. Sometimes it took them a month or two to soften him up, but in the end he could be fleeced of millions, a farmhouse, a piece of land, even a tractor.

When someone in a neighbouring village hanged himself after losing his vineyard, Matteo decided to stop the games. Now there was nothing in the room but a game of table football and an ice cream freezer.

Corso found Elena turned towards the coffee machine, the triangle of her back defined by the apron round her waist. Matteo was behind the window in the lotto cubby-hole, his bald head surrounded by coupons and scratch cards.

"Phone call," Elena said, without turning round.

The telephone was on the corridor wall near the toilets. These had modern round seats that overlooked a bank of violets in spring, so that anyone standing up to pee would see the rocks and smell the flowers. The best time was in the morning or at sunset, when the rays of the sun were nearly horizontal and glorified the hills with an aura. This caused extraordinarily long visits to the toilet. Everyone knew about it, but it was never mentioned in the bar. A woman would undoubtedly have mentioned it, and so perhaps would a writer, but no woman had noticed it because they squatted and the only local writer, a dialect poet in a foulard neckerchief, had died several years before without referring to the subject.

Corso picked up the receiver.

It was Arcadipane. "Nice life for those free to spend their mornings in bars."

"Yes. Well?"

"Talking to you is always so satisfying."

"Of course. Go on."

"The results have come through."

"And?"

"You remember those were the earliest days of D.N.A.?"

"Yes."

"And you insisted on collecting samples even so?"

"I did."

"Well, just as well you never listened to me."

Corso looked at the retired schoolteacher sitting at the table by the door. She was reading a collection of the tragedies of Alfieri, nursing her second small glass of white wine.

"Corso?"

During the last sixty years the woman had taught everyone in the district in the top class at primary school, including him. Now she spent her mornings in the bar, and her afternoons in a little room at the library where no-one else ever went.

"Corso?"

He looked the clock above the schoolteacher. 10.18. A time for finding people in the bar once successful in doing something they do no longer.

"I'm coming," Corso finally said.

13

"Farmapex?"

"Good evening, Margit."

"Signor Monticelli, good evening!"

"I have to ask you a favour. Please book me a seat on the first flight tomorrow to Bucharest."

"I'll do it at once. Today I rang Signor Richt for . . ."

"Just make a note of that, I'll see about it when I get back."

"Certainly, Signor Monticelli"

"For the air ticket, Margit, use the agency that just booked me a hotel."

"But we have our own . . ."

"I know, but this time I'd like it this way."

"Of course, Signor Monticelli, I'll call them at once."

"Thank you. What can you see from the window?"

"Sorry?"

"Your office overlooks the garden. Are the street lamps lit yet?"

"They've just come on. It's been a grey day here, quite dark."

"What can you see?"

"The bench where you often sit, the hedge . . ."

"Has it been trimmed?"

"Yesterday."

"What else?"

"Now the tree has lost nearly all its flowers."

"None left?"

"I don't think so but, as you directed, the gardener hasn't cleared them away."

". . ."

"Signor Monticelli?"

"You've been very kind, Margit, I'll let you go home now."

"But Signor Monticelli, I still haven't . . ."

"Go home, the day's over and you have children. Just arrange that ticket . . ."

"I'll see to it instantly."

"Goodnight, Margit."

"Goodnight, Signor Monticelli."

14

"Could there be some mistake?"

Arcadipane shook his head. "How long did you work here?"

"Twelve years," Corso said.

"And in that time, how often did they blunder?"

"Twice."

"Add twice more since you left, let's say four times in thirty years. That's a good record for a lab, surely?"

Corso looked down at the page again without disagreeing. But Arcadipane knew well that habit of smoothing his beard with one finger.

"Holy Christ!" he snorted, reaching for the phone and pressing an internal number.

"Send up Sabbatini," he said into the phone.

He put it down, opened a drawer, lit a cigarette and dropped the packet on top of the pile of folders on his desk. The ashtray was half full and as usual his office was cloaked in smoke. But the heat was bearable: after a squall at midday the sun had got back to work, though probably too late to regain lost ground before evening.

While Corso was rereading the report, there came a knock on the door.

"Come in," Arcadipane said.

The woman in shapeless trousers, jeans shirt and black

trainers looked as if she had been interrupted while tidying a garage. She came in without opening the door fully. Fat, with short frizzy hair and glasses, she had the sort of face you only notice on the stairs or in a shop if you have tooth-ache.

"Our D.N.A. expert," Arcadipane said. "Whenever people in Rome can't get a spider out of its hole, they send for Sabbatini. Sabbatini, this pain in the arse is Bramard."

Corso made a sign of acknowledgement without getting up, while the woman looked from the sandals on his feet to the papers in his hand.

"We were just talking about that hair I sent you," Arcadipane said.

The woman made no attempt to hide how bored she clearly felt at having to return to a problem she considered solved. Not someone likely to have too many friends. Corso imagined evenings alone at home with the microwave, portions for one, and puzzles.

"I told him," Arcadipane said, "but he doesn't trust south-erners. Where are you from?"

"Macerata," the woman said.

"Could be worse, perhaps you can convince him."

The woman was chewing something. There was a casual side to her, certainly, but a touch of distinction too.

"What do I have to explain?" she said.

Corso looked at her more carefully. He had already annoyed her, so he could not do much worse. Her bull neck and cheeks covered with faint hairs did her no favours, but she could not have been much over thirty.

"I'd like to know how you came to your conclusion," he said.

"I don't draw conclusions . . ."

"Stop!" Arcadipane interrupted her. "Let's not argue about

which of us is the more sensitive, O.K.? Tell him what you told me and let's leave it at that, I need to go out to do some damned on-the-spot investigating."

The woman took a breath. She did not seem disturbed. There was a little dandruff on her shoulders, and she was wearing a child's watch.

"The hair was not torn out, but cut off," she said, so it has no root. That limits what we can extract from it, but an analysis of the mitochondrial D.N.A. could still yield some information, for example about descent in the maternal line."

She stopped. Corso nodded to show he understood.

"So I compared the D.N.A. of the hair with the samples we have in the archive concentrating on comparisons of this kind. It resulted in a correspondence with the D.N.A. of the first victim ..." She fixed her grey eyes on the ashtray.

"Clara Pontremoli," Corso suggested.

"Clara Pontremoli."

Corso looked back at the papers. Arcadipane watched him, wishing above all else that he would stop rubbing his beard with his finger.

"Say a bit more about the mother," he said finally.

The woman went on. "The hair is unquestionably from a blood relative of the mother of Clara Pontremoli, which means it could have come from Clara Pontremoli herself or a brother or sister of hers, or from the children of a sister of her mother, that is to say a male or female cousin.

She scratched her cheek. Probably no-one had ever told her what a masculine gesture this was.

"But in this case, since there are no cousins because Clara's mother had no sisters, and Clara's brother Gregorio died in a car accident in Greece in 1983, the only person the hair could have come from is Clara Pontremoli herself."

The office was heavy with the silence that follows a long piece of reasoning, rather like the sound of a wheel continuing to spin in the air after a bicycle has fallen into a ditch.

"Is it possible to establish when the hair was cut?" Corso said.

"No," the woman said. "There's no way to do that."

"So it could date from the time of the rape?"

"Meaning?"

"About twenty-five years ago."

"If preserved with care to inhibit deterioration."

"What sort of care?"

"A plastic envelope or a moisture-proof container. Even a dry drawer might do."

Corso slid one piece of paper under another. Then he read a bit more, stopped stroking his beard and closed the folder.

"Thank you, Sabbatini," Arcadipane said. "You may go."

The woman went out, leaving behind her the smell of a train compartment. Corso massaged his ankle. His dry bony feet had large raised veins, and the leather of his sandals was like desiccated flesh.

"Well?" Arcadipane said.

For many years he had been forced to put up with Commissario Bramard's silences, in the hope that they might lead to something. Now he had a right to interrupt as soon as he had had enough – in other words, almost immediately.

Corso uncrossed and recrossed his legs and began massaging the other ankle.

"When did they find the Pontremoli woman?" he asked.

Arcadipane lit another cigarette.

"In February '81. You must look at the file for the exact day, but I remember the month because I had just put in my request for a transfer. And you?"

"I'd just taken the exam for commissario."

"I've always asked myself how come they made you a commissario when you were a communist."

"I've never been a communist."

"Really?"

"No."

"What were you, then?"

"Action Party."

"What action?"

Corso shook his head that it didn't matter and started stroking his cheek with the back of his index finger again. Arcadipane scrutinised him between puffs, surreptitiously trying to read what anyone would have seen as two barricaded eyes in a face locked shut.

When Arcadipane had discovered that in Turin he would be joining the team of someone called Bramard, he made a few enquiries. "Well done," his colleagues said, "but you certainly won't have a lot of laughs."

The first time they had met, Bramard had been reading a book in court. He had waited for someone to be released before speaking. "Sit down," he had said, "this could take some time." And so it was: two and a half hours without a single word or even a coffee. Then the commissario had closed his book. "I don't strike, I don't blackmail, I don't threaten and I'm not inclined to spare people," he had said. "In fact you're going to be bored – you should know that from the start. If that doesn't suit you, you can ask for a transfer while there's still time." He had then gone back to his book.

What this meant became clear in the first few weeks. You just had to get used to it and he had done so and soon they were cooperating like a horse and an ox harnessed to the same yoke.

Now Arcadipane watched the ash lengthen on his cigarette. He laid it carefully on the ashtray and glanced at Bramard's wooden face. It had been a long time since they last worked together, but reading the other's mind was something he would never unlearn.

"Do you believe he has been keeping that hair all these years?" he said.

Corso's snort shook his lips. A very French way of snorting. He had been doing this for so long that he could not remember when and where he had learnt it. Just as well for him.

"She was the first one he attacked and the only one he left alive. Perhaps that should have interested us more."

"When they passed the case on to us we read all the reports, didn't we?" Arcadipane exclaimed, spreading his arms wide. "And we went to interview her more than once."

"Twice."

"It could just as well have been ten times. In the state she was in it was impossible to get anything out of her."

"It was two years after the event."

"The report said it was the same when they found her."

Women could be heard shouting in the corridor in some unknown language. Corso gestured with his chin. Arcadipane shook his head: routine pavement round-up. Corso let his eyes rest on a photograph album on the desk. There was a small hourglass on the retailer's sticker on the album.

"Where is she now?" he asked,

"The Pontremoli woman? How the fuck do I know?"

Corso stared at him. Outside the door some kind of bargaining involving a number of people seemed to be in progress. Arcadipane held his look for a moment, then took an unnaturally short pull on his cigarette before picking up his telephone. He ignored the first words from the other end.

"Buozzi? Why are those women in the corridor?"

He closed his face.

"What fucking interrogation?! Do me a favour, take a sheet of paper and ask them one at a time how many they had last night and where, sign the whole thing and fax it to the questore."

Silence.

"What fucking Excel?! Send them away. This is a job where you need to use your brain. I want silence!"

Replacing the phone, the commissario relaxed into his chair. The voices in the corridor continued for a while, then several said, "Shhhh," and heels could be heard getting further away. Arcadipane studied the grey spirals rising from his cigarette.

"And after that," he said, "she was in the Cottolengo. And not a comma has been changed."

"She didn't go back home?"

"Who to? Her mother – after what happened – threw herself off a balcony. Her brother killed himself in his car in Greece. Her father died of a heart attack in '91. End of the happy Pontremoli family."

"Was there no-one else?"

"A brother of her father, but he had been living in Libya for more than forty years. He had no children and was working with gas concessions. He only came back to Italy for the funerals of his brother and sister-in-law."

Corso went back to gazing at the hourglass on the back of the photograph album. It was beautifully designed. Not easy to do a better job than that with only seven strokes of the pen.

"Will you give me permission?" he said.

"For what?"

"To go and see her."

Arcadipane stared at the door behind which, now the shouting of the women had gone, nothing to be heard but the familiar voices of his subordinates with their ill-humour, their obtuseness, their sweat, their wit, their occasional diploma (an endemic case of corruption), their heaps of papers, their hormones, their ovulations, their debts, their holsters, their weapons, their protocols, their gambling; and a last obstinate foggy surviving illusion.

Then he leaned his head back gently against the headrest, as if offering his neck to a barber or an executioner.

"This work is shit," he said. "It doesn't grip me anymore, you know."

15

Corso was sitting waiting when the door opened and a nun of about sixty came in, accompanied by a little of the wind that had been assaulting the city for the last three days, threatening rain without fulfilling that promise. The nun's habit was black and threadbare, her stockings grey.

She introduced herself: "I'm Suor Luciana."

Corso shook her hand, realising he had never touched a nun before.

"Bramard."

Suor Luciana walked round the desk and sat down with her hands in her lap. But for a crucifix, a calendar dedicated to the Virgin Mary and an olive branch on the wall, the room could easily have been the registry office of a small town.

"If anyone asks to see one of our daughters," she said, smiling, "it is our custom to look favourably on the idea. A person offering friendship without ulterior motives can only be beneficial. And the visitor nearly always comes to realise that it is he who has profited the most."

Corso studied the nun closely. She must be of peasant stock, thus intelligent but used to not showing it: a woman capable of giving orders without the arrogance common to those accustomed to being in command. But she had the habit of command too, there could be no doubt about that. Her small eyes were unattractive, but she had lips of great beauty. Impossible to imagine what she must have been like as a girl.

"I am the commissario once responsible for investigating the case of Clara Pontremoli," Corso said. Suor Luciana nodded maternally. She knew perfectly well who he was and also, perhaps, why he was there: after all, matters of conscience were her profession.

Corso looked out of the window at the courtyard. To pass the time before their appointment, he had measured the distance round the building: 2,148 paces, a good kilometre of brick without antechambers, balconies or neutral areas. Nothing to create any doubt about what was inside and what was outside. Perhaps this was why, even though they were at the heart of the noise, commerce and filth of the city, everything seemed quiet and under control. The price for this was a certain lack of oxygen.

"It's rather hot, don't you find?" Suor Luciana said.

She went to the window and opened one side of it, and raised a hand to greet someone outside that Corso could not see.

"Clara," she said without turning round, "is one of our most difficult daughters, and so one of the most loved. You must not expect too much from her."

Corso looked down at his sandals. The leather over his toes was faded, as if they had been worn by someone who had been waiting for years at the edge of the sea, his shoes gradually salted by the waves.

"I shall bear that in mind," he said.

They crossed the yard, skirted a low building, then passed through a second yard, a colonnade and a hexagonal area where several visitors were playing with a soft ball under the supervision of a friar. Every so often electric rickshaws interrupted their progress, forcing them to stop briefly until they trundled off with their loads of laundry, reheated meals or rubbish bins.

But no sounds hinted at the people who must need all this.

They entered a building with five storeys, walked up two extremely clean flights of stairs and knocked on the door of what seemed likely to be a flat.

The door was opened by a girl of South American appearance.

Suor Luciana introduced her: "Rosaria from Peru, one of our educators."

"Good morning," the girl said.

Behind her, in a large living room, five women were watching "Murder, She Wrote" on television. Some were older than others, but all were wearing the same clothes and had their hair piled on top of their heads and held in place with brown hairpins and the occasional rubber band.

"We have a visitor!" the Peruvian girl announced in a loud voice.

Only one of the women turned. Her eyes, blue and full of snow, studied the newcomer. A Russian poet who survived the Gulag, Corso thought as the woman turned back to watch the screen, almost as if unmasked.

"I'll tell Clara there's someone to see her," Suor Luciana said, going off down a corridor, opening one of the first doors and disappearing inside.

"A glass of water?" the girl asked Corso. "Or some fruit juice?"

She had long black hair tucked behind exceptionally beautiful ears, and skin of almost diabolical perfection.

Corso gave a half-smile as if to say, "Please don't take the trouble." A couple of steps took him to the window. Beyond the grille he could see the road with his car parked by the pavement, two trees and the façades of a large building and a church.

As with us all there had been a time when beauty had entered him spontaneously, but that had been in his earlier life, the time when he was innocent and could believe in anything, before he discovered that beauty always conceals something irretrievable. Since then, his reaction to beauty had always been a half-smile and "Please don't take the trouble." Elena was the only exception.

"Excuse me!"

He turned. The Russian poet was hugging the Peruvian girl, her head buried in the girl's breast.

"I'm so sorry," the girl said. "But that's Camilla's place. She doesn't like it when anyone else takes it from her."

Corso moved away from the window.

"Look!" the girl said to the poet. "Now there's no-one there anymore!"

The woman, who on her feet was seen to be short and quite round, darted a doubtful look over her shoulder, then shuffled in her slippers to the window, took a notebook and pencil from the pocket of her trousers and made some sort of note. Meanwhile Jessica Fletcher was explaining in detail to the four still on the sofa who had committed the murder and why.

Corso looked at the Peruvian educator, who smiled.

"This is how she passes nearly all her time," she said. "She writes if it's raining, if a dog or bicycle passes, what time they sweep the street, if someone stops to talk or goes to throw rubbish away. She has a wardrobe full of those notebooks. We tried taking them away from her, but . . ." She made a gesture as if to say "God forbid!" "I think she's been doing it for years."

"Commissario!" Suor Luciana was calling him.

Corso entered the corridor leading to the room of the only witness he had been able to meet for twenty-five years.

"Clara's not used to visitors," Suor Luciana said at the door. "Speak calmly without raising your voice, and don't touch her.

She doesn't like to be touched. If you see her getting nervous, say goodbye quietly and come out. I'll come in with you."

When Corso agreed to this, the nun pushed open the door and stood aside.

Clara was lying on top of the bedclothes, her pillow raised against the headboard and eyes fixed on the wardrobe opposite. The blind was drawn, and there was very little light from the outside.

"Come and sit down," Suor Luciana said, taking a towel off one of the two chairs.

"Good morning," Corso said.

All the woman did was move her eyes to three little bonsai trees on the windowsill. The rest of her meagre figure stayed motionless in her too-large tracksuit. Her breasts were small like those of all the victims. Like Michelle's.

The televised mayhem of a chase intruded from the living room. "It's over!" someone shouted. "The house is surrounded!"

Corso's eyes moved down to the beautiful white feet of Clara Pontremoli. She had lost five toes.

16

The razor blade travelled over skin stretched by the light twist-ing of Jean-Claude's neck. A familiar and intuitive journey. The silky sound of laceration was like the stem of a plant being cut lengthwise along its vascular channel. A little slower to prepare for a change of angle before the long stretch to the cheekbone. Someone knocked.

Jean-Claude wiped the last traces of foam from his face. He examined his handiwork, and was satisfied.

Leaving the bathroom, he made his way round the luggage at the foot of the bed, and stooped to pick up the piece of paper someone had pushed in under the door.

He read it, then went to the phone and called reception.

"Monticelli," he said. "Cancel my flight, send a barley coffee up to my room with some spelt bread, together with a map of the city."

At that moment a thermostat switched on the heating in his room. Jean-Claude picked up the tie he had left on the bed and placed it on one of the freshly folded shirts.

"No, there's no special hurry, thank you."

17

The woman's lightless eyes continued to stare at the bonsai.

Her head was no longer shaved as it had been after three weeks of captivity, when photographed by the team who had found her twenty-five years before, nor was it as short as when, two years later, Corso and Arcadipane had gone to interview the woman now lying on the bed after the passage of another twenty-three years.

"A lot of time has passed," Corso said. "I do realise that."

On February 16, 1981 an anonymous letter had directed the police to the hut in the woods where Clara Pontremoli had been found naked, chained by the ankle with five toes amputated, and in a state of shock. During the next few days examinations had ruled out drugs and sexual violence, and estimated that her wounds would need fifteen days to heal. In fact the incisions on her back had already been sutured by the aggressor himself with a firm if unprofessional hand, at points where the blade had been pressed in too deep (a mistake a more experienced Autumnal would not repeat). And her feet had been medicated.

"The forensic people have given us some information at long last. That's why I've come now to ask you a few questions."

Leaves had blown into the hut, where there had also been plates, glasses, a saucepan, two frying pans and three empty

French wine bottles. There were no fingerprints, and no trace of tyres even outside the hut where the man had walked, knowing the leaves would not preserve his footprints. No-one who had been in the woods at the time had heard cries or been aware of the presence of strangers.

"I'd like you to answer, please, even if only to say yes or no."

Under one of the two camp beds they had also found a pail, a bottle of shampoo, some perfume, a hairbrush and the shears the attacker had used to cut off Clara Pontremoli's toes and also her hair, just as he was to do later with his other victims. Hanging on the wall had been the nylon cord he had used to immobilise her while this was being done.

To begin with, the investigation had concentrated on the private life of the victim, starting with her emotional history. No-one imagined a serial attack until the second woman was violated and her corpse discovered – thanks to a second anonymous letter – in an almost identical hiding-place, surrounded by the same objects and with similar incisions in her back.

The same procedure was repeated five more times, for women like Pontremoli who were between twenty-five and thirty-two years old, tall and slim, with small breasts and long black hair. The method was always the same: abduction, no demand for ransom, the victim discovered thanks to a letter sent to the police a few weeks later, found with the same incisions on her back and amputated toes. Unlike Clara Pontremoli, found alive, all the others had had their throats cut and their blood drained into a white plastic tub. The last had been Michelle.

Corso looked at the woman before him, her hands lying in her lap as if forgotten. Beautiful with a beauty only too familiar to him.

"You went into that hut knowing full well what would happen, didn't you?"

77

Clara Pontremoli continued to stare at the windowsill. Saliva trickled from the corner of her mouth. Suor Luciana reached out to dry it with her handkerchief.

"I don't think this—"

"Please sit down," Corso said.

"The agreement was that—"

"Put away that handkerchief and sit down."

The nun held his gaze for a moment, then sat down. Corso continued to stare at Clara Pontremoli. Now saliva was running down to her chest from closed lips.

"Perhaps you never imagined other demands would be made of you or that he could have got to the point of killing, but you did know what he was looking for. How long had you been playing the game?"

The woman turned her head for the first time and looked into Corso's eyes.

When he was a child and there had been dogs in the house, Corso's was a female wolfhound called Sparta. She was partly descended from Czechoslovakian wolves and didn't mix with other dogs. He was very fond of her. They would often go out with other local boys, and when the boys started their long battles with stones or swords, the wolfhound would sit high up and a little apart to watch, as she would have done with cubs in the pack, only intervening if a boy was reduced to tears when hit by a stone or a well-aimed blow from a wooden sword.

One day, when Sparta was asleep on the front steps at home, Corso had lifted a foot to step over her, but the wolf-hound, perhaps waking from a dream in which she or her cubs were threatened, had suddenly closed her teeth round his calf.

Corso had not cried out or felt any pain because she had not pierced his skin, but he had seen the dog's eyes fixed on him full of fear and self-hate. Then she had urinated on herself and gone to hide in the garage.

Corso recognised the same fear and rage in Clara's eyes. An instant later she threw her head back and hurled herself violently against the wall.

"Help!" Suor Luciana cried, trying to keep hold of Clara and pull the cord of the alarm at the same time.

Corso did not move. Clara Pontremoli banged her head on the wall again and again.

When the Peruvian educator and two nurses threw open the door and flung themselves at the bed, Corso was staring at a bloodstain on the wall.

The sequence of his thoughts at that moment was astonishingly syllogistic, considering the uproar.

It had started as a game, initially innocent like all games, to show Autumnal the path to beauty he had been searching for. After which a subtle intelligence, a nature devoted to completeness and lacking moral scruples had led him to pursue the most exact details, until he had made himself their master.

But one thing still needed to be explained: why did he ever stop? Why give up what had enabled him to fulfil his talent? Certainly not from fear of being caught or from remorse. Perhaps a greater pleasure, a more profound and more lasting beauty?

By the time Corso emerged from these thoughts, Clara Pontremoli was lying sedated on the bed, with her back towards him and half-naked after her great agitation. The two nurses and the educator were watching her, panting for breath, their hands suddenly empty.

"Come to my office," Suor Luciana said, tidying the hair which had slipped out from under her veil. She had a red scratch on her cheek.

Before leaving the room, Corso took a long look at Clara Pontremoli's scars. They were less exact than the scars on Michelle's back had been. Autumnal's apprenticeship had been just beginning.

But even so, they were extremely beautiful.

18

"Your behaviour was appalling," Suor Luciana said as soon as she was able to relax in her chair. "And after I warned you that of all our daughters she was one of the most . . ." Now a fresh wind was blowing in horizontally from the office window. "I could have refused to let you see her, but I trusted you." The interrogative tail of a cat could be seen dancing beyond the low wall outside. "I was sure you would know how to behave. Such a thing has never happened before."

The cat suddenly jumped into view: it was large and rather slow, ginger and white. Corso studied it with the rage and envy dogs feel for cats, but cats never feel for dogs.

"Have you no interest at all in what I'm saying? Doesn't the suffering of that woman concern you in any way?"

Corso turned his eyes to the nun.

"When may it have happened before?" he said.

"I don't understand." Suor Luciana shook her head.

All the green had vanished from Corso's eyes, leaving only the old metallic grey that was fundamental to them behind the patina of the milder shade.

"You said such a thing has never happened before. When may such a thing have happened before?"

Suor Luciana took her hands from the desk and placed them in her lap one on top of the other like a priest or a pregnant woman.

"I don't know, when the man who was her friend at university came to see her."

"What friend?"

"I thought . . ."

"What is his name?"

"How on earth can I remember?" She put her hands back on the desk. "He comes each year on Christmas Eve . . . Always brings one of those plants."

"Are you there when they meet?"

"Of course, but nothing happens that . . ." She searched for a word she could not find. "He only stays a few minutes and talks to her about their time at university, and obviously gets no answer."

"Describe him to me."

"A very distinguished man, about fifty, tall, grizzled. His clothes . . ."

"His clothes?"

"A bit . . . I wouldn't say eccentric, but not like a businessman's, even if that's what he looks like. Special, there."

Corso looked out of the window. The cat was licking its belly. To do this it had had to stick one of its paws up in a rather unseemly manner.

"When I came in I had to sign a register. Is that always the case?"

"All visitors sign."

"And are the registers kept?"

"You are asking me . . ."

"It's important."

Suor Luciana touched her cheek. It was perhaps only now that she realised she had been scratched.

"I'd have to ask," she said.

Corso turned towards her. Suor Luciana looked at him as

one might look at someone already far from humanity and from everything that makes living among human beings bearable.

"You've never stopped being a policeman, have you?"

Corso turned back to look for the cat. It had gone. The first great drops of dust and stratosphere exploded in the courtyard.

"If you abandoned your veil, would you no longer be a nun?"

19

Jean-Claude Monticelli parked the car he had hired, a low-powered Japanese model, in the yard of the old brick factory. He folded the small map that had guided him through the labyrinth of fields, picked up his overnight case and got out.

The factory was a brick building with a factory chimney shaped like a cone, a kiln and two more recent sheds roofed in Eternit asbestos, all long abandoned. Windows, gutters, drainpipes and electric cables had been looted, though the surviving mixture of naked walls, vegetation and metal looked entirely natural.

He pulled on his gloves and breathed the atmosphere of peaceful ruin. Since dawn the sky had seemed covered by a sheet of ashes. In a line of poplars, a few birds were trying and failing to compete with the murmur of the river.

Walking almost on tiptoe to keep the hems of his trousers from the mud, he headed for the great half-open door of the factory. Anticipating the probable condition of the place, he had put on the shoes he kept for hunting expeditions. He had a pair of soft Swedish buckskin moccasins ready on the back seat of the car.

He slid back the factory door, big enough to admit lorries, and went in. The interior was large, well-lit and now luxuriant with ivy, ready to be photographed for some piece of research into industrial archaeology.

Monticelli made his way to the ladder leading up to the raised office where some loyal servant, watching through the glass walls, had once supervised loading and unloading.

When he came into the room, the man sitting behind the desk was smiling and relaxed, but with the shadows under his eyes of someone who had enjoyed a series of late nights. Even his clothes did not look professional: bright blue, showy and cheaply cut.

He was also wearing a lot of gold, something Monticelli only found acceptable on fat men and black women, while this man, who was about forty years old, was of a classic Slav build with a cheeky, good-looking appearance not too badly marked by cocaine (nostrils with broken capillaries) and gambling (excessively well cared-for nails).

The man held out his hand in a cordial manner, indicating the chair in front of the desk with the same gesture as his colleague of the previous day – perhaps a trademark of the firm.

Monticelli looked at the chair to make sure it was clean before sitting down. By the time he got up again, the man had already pushed the folder towards him.

"Was the girl in the hotel alright?" he said.

Monticelli picked up the folder and leafed through it.

It contained eight girls, as he had asked, all slim and vaguely blonde, photographed in swimsuits and evening dress. Underneath each was her name, city of origin and academic qualifications (one even had a degree from an English university). On the back of each page were sayings attributed to the girls (*What pleases you pleases me*), a passport number and a photocopy of a medical certificate as evidence that she had been tested for A.I.D.S. and other venereal diseases.

"How soon can they be in Switzerland?" Monticelli said.

The man smiled. "If we pay now, next week. No problem at all." He spread his hands to show how easy it was.

"Good," Monticelli said, still running his eye over the infinite variations of blonde available in girls from eastern Europe. "But first I need proof that you really are Adrian."

The man laughed and started swinging in his chair, which was not made for swinging. The floor was littered with broken glass and pages from newspapers and old magazines printed in sober Soviet characters. He stopped swinging but went on laughing as he took a passport from the inside pocket of his jacket and threw it down on the table.

Monticelli flicked through it, then slipped it into his own pocket.

Adrian stopped laughing. Two legs of his chair were still off the ground in a sort of vigilant expectation.

Monticelli held up the palm of his hand as if to indicate a mere formality, then opened the overnight case on his lap.

The snap of its two small locks seemed to reassure the Romanian, who lowered the legs of his chair and leaned back.

Monticelli gave him a reassuring smile, then lowered his eyes to busy himself inside the suitcase. When he had finished he closed the case, raised his arm with the silenced pistol and placed a small bullet in the centre of his interlocutor's forehead. It was as simple as a coin falling innocuously into a fountain.

Adrian's eyes stayed wide open. His lips seemed to have stopped in the middle of a word he was suddenly uncertain of.

The hole on his forehead was no bigger than a cherry stone and very little blood came out of it.

Monticelli unscrewed the silencer and put it back in the case together with the pistol, fastening both in with suitable pieces of Velcro, before taking a notebook from his jacket pocket and drawing a line through the first item in a list of five.

When he noticed Adrian's body beginning to slip to one side, he put away the notebook, stretched forward and, careful not to brush the dusty desk with his tie, propped him upright again.

Then he took a Polaroid camera out of his suitcase and the newspaper he had bought a little earlier before going into the car-hire firm.

20

Cross the garden under the early afternoon sun, follow the gravel path as far as the small art nouveau building, and go inside. Hurry up the stairs two at a time though aware that it is still early, to reach the second floor, where the door to the landing is closed and the corridor immersed in the silence of their sleep.

Sit on the bench, your knees to your chest, your back against the little windcheaters and coats on the hangers. Stare into the darkness where they are sleeping, smile at the smell of the food they have been eating, and at the named cloth bags containing their bathing things. Then hear a little song coming from the end of the corridor: "*Gaston, y a le téléphone qui sonne,*" turn and recognise her small figure facing the wall, and the little apron tied round her waist with parcel string.

Ask yourself, "Why parcel string?" as you get up and go over to her.

"*Et y a jamais personne qui . . .*"

Ask her, "What are you doing here all on your own?" as you caress her. "Let's go home!" And at the same moment you become aware that her hair is coming away from her head in handfuls, and that the acid smell emanating from her little body is like a cancer, a cry, or a badly spoken farewell.

Corso stared at his empty fingers, much used and covered with scars. His hands were the only thing about him that anyone would have found remarkable. Remarkable to the extent that his father had passed them on to him; though what he had done since and was still doing now was another matter.

They knocked again.

He got up from the armchair where he had waited for the night hours to pass and went to the door.

"Come in," he said.

He put on the coffee and as he was doing so threw a glance at the clock on the dresser. Just after eight. His uncle had parked the sack beside his chair and was wearing his grey tracksuit. On Thursday mornings he had his yoga course.

"Have you seen the Romanian woman?" he asked.

Corso was not surprised by the lack of preamble. It had been the same when he was a child and his uncle had come to collect him from boarding school at Mondovì, telling him to hurry and pack his things because his father had been hit by a hail of shot while hunting.

A few hours later they were at the hospital where the man was lying in a room with three beds, all occupied by people who would not go home again. During the few minutes he was allowed to see his father he had been in a restless state, as in the afternoons when he fell asleep on the sofa, interrupted by starts during which he opened his eyes wide without seeing anything, the only moments when he had ever seemed like other men, familiar with doubt and guilt.

Corso, however, during the few minutes he spent in the room, had not thought about this at all, but as always happens in hospital wards had been distracted by banal and unfamiliar things like the drip, the bad smell, the people in the neighbouring beds, whether or not to touch his father, the urine, and everything else.

His mother had kept silent, one hand on her husband's

forearm where a big X and a skull with a rose in its mouth had been tattooed. Corso did not understand what these meant, but he had heard them mentioned locally with both scorn and reverence. After all, he was only nine years old and in that bed was a man who loved in the distant and contentious manner in which one can love the mountain that all your life has closed the horizon of your valley. He had spent the next hours in the corridor, both sides of it lined with men who had come for various reasons to wait in silence for somebody else's last breath. A silence that had exhausted him, like farewells heavy with unspoken words.

In the weeks that followed the funeral he had regained his strength, lost the habit of prayer that had weighed so heavily on his schooldays and begun to spend time, at first hesitantly and then openly, at his uncle's house, a place put out of bounds during his father's lifetime by an unspoken veto.

He and his uncle never found it difficult to understand one another, and right from the start had not communicated in words. Thus, without any official declarations and with the silent consent of his mother, his uncle had come to be a father to him first, then a brother, and finally, had it not been for the reticence that regulated relations between men in their world, Corso would have said that they had become friends.

There had only been two occasions when they had needed anything more than a look to understand one another, The first had been when Corso was sixteen and his uncle had told him why he had been given that name, and the second when Corso at twenty had told his uncle that he wanted to join the police.

"I've done what I had to," was all his uncle had said on that occasion, implying that he had detached the boy from the priests and brought him to the present point in his life to the best of his ability.

The coffee took time. Corso rinsed out the pot.

"I told her about it the other evening," he said. "She'd like a month before answering."

His uncle nodded. From outside the distant wheeze of a tractor could be heard under the gurgling of the coffee. Corso carried the two cups and the sugar to the table.

"Have you still got that old Luger?"

His uncle took his usual spoonful.

"I have."

"Does it work?"

"Depends."

The telephone rang. Corso went over to it. It was Arcadipane.

"Want the good news first or the bad?"

"Up to you."

"According to the handwriting analysis, the signature in the registers and the letter are in the same hand, so the man who goes to the Cottolengo must be our man."

"And the bad news?"

"There are three people with that name: one's in a wheel-chair, one's a boy of fourteen, and one is a lawyer in Padua who was seven years old at the time of the relevant events. So the name's a false one. End of story."

"Have you checked abroad?"

"Nothing."

A ray of sun had come round the corner of the window, marking out a blade on the floor.

"But we have the identikit, when he comes again . . ."

"He won't come again," Corso said.

"But been coming for the last seven years!"

"He won't come again, Corso repeated.

For a moment he went on staring at the tiny volatile frag-ments of dust in the corridor of sunlight. Was there any order in their agitation? To understand it did one need to share their microscopic nature or rise to a level higher than the merely physical?

"What do you need the Luger for?" his uncle asked.

Corso went back to his coffee.

"Nothing."

21

"If you want to do this job properly," a colleague nearing retirement had told him during one of his first cases, "don't be so stupid as to go around showing off your police badge like a lot of those idiots do, or people will just get scared and either watch what they say or start acting and putting on a performance, which is even worse. Better to find a quiet place like this, park yourself a chair in front of the window, and prepare to be patient."

It did not take Corso long to realise that, seen like that, it was the right career for him.

In fact the only two activities he had ever shown any aptitude for, ever since he'd been a child, had been watching life from the sidelines and reading, which after all is much the same thing. Two occupations which, pursued with the abnegation of his first twenty years, had already made him conscious as a young man of a truth that only comes to most people with the disenchantment of age.

A bitter truth, but very useful for an investigator. The human comedy, however varied it may seem at first sight, shows itself if studied with detachment to be very like the "periodic table" of elements with which Mendeleev tried to summarise the world.

Enough to say that a limited number of impulses such as jealousy, greed, abandon, pride, lust, hate, humiliation, courage, envy, love, desire, ambition, revenge, a sense of omnipotence and more combine to generate the totality of human actions, whether noble or ignoble, memorable or trivial, commonplace or extraordinary.

Then, on what are fortunately comparatively rare occasions, one of these combinations will produce a murder.

This was where Corso came in. Given a death, he would go back to the mixture of impulses that had produced it. In his eyes, this was how to find the culprit. A craft consisting of logic, observation and a knowledge of its elements. Work in which words did not count for much, since the elements in question had been operating long before human beings had anything to say or any way of saying it. In fact, a job to be done sitting in front of the window, because if you want to understand a battle, the last place you want to be standing is in the middle of it. Better to keep your distance on higher ground, as his colleague had advised, away from the shouts and the clash of arms.

It was from this high ground that, wrapped in the combination of admiration and diffidence with which all those who have talent are seen, he had climbed the ranks of the police to become the youngest commissario in Italy.

But then, one day, the questore had placed the yellow and already well-thumbed folder of the Autumnal case on his desk.

"Will you take it on?" the questore had asked.

All he then knew about the case was what he had read in the press and picked up in the corridors. The questore, in charge until the previous day, had not been unprepared. Maybe a little short of imagination, but a good worker if rather old-fashioned, with well-worn shoes and a quick manner, capable both of smooth talk and of raising his voice; if he had got nowhere it had been because of a more or less anomalous and seductive combination of elements.

"Alright," Corso had agreed.

And when the questore had left the room, Corso had taken a piece of paper and written in pencil: *Why women? Why without blood? Why the marks? Is the murderer talking to himself or to others? An open series or a fixed number? Are autumn and winter relevant? Any sexual sequence?* And then lower down: *Photos of the women. Photos of the huts. Maps. Talk to the survivor. Forensic reports. Relatives of the victims. Lives of the victims (Arcadipane). The places. Change the name of the folder – "Autumnal" could be misleading.*

A year after he had made all these suggestions to himself, all these things had been done apart from the last one, but none of the questions had been answered. And the number of women killed had risen to five. All between autumn and winter.

Sometimes, during the investigations, he had felt he was getting warmer, but it had always proved to be a distant light from some detail too isolated to let him grasp any overall pattern. But there was a pattern, he was sure of that. And he was certain it was a big pattern, well-thought-out and developed.

Where was he going wrong? Was the high ground too far away? Or too near? Or did the periodic table he had always trusted lack some essential element?

Then, one night, while he was setting his thoughts in good order on his office desk, the battle he had assumed to be elsewhere had silently moved up to his high place, knocking at his own door and swallowing up Michelle and Martina. After this, drowning in the blood and pain he had always previously only contemplated from a distance, he had become incapable of lucidity and firmness. He had abandoned the field. Abandoning them and, after that, abandoning himself. And losing everything.

"Professor Bramard?"

Corso lifted his eyes from the sheet of paper on which he had been scribbling for the last half-hour.

"We've reached the vote, Professor Bramard," said a colleague. "Do you agree to exclusion for a single day without compulsory attendance?"

Corso raised his hand, like most of the others in the room. There was a certain amount of mumbling, after which the decision was entered in the minutes and the meeting adjourned. During the noise of chairs being moved, Corso went back to staring at the network of lines which still after many years effectively concealed the secret of a principal planner.

"Since when have you been in favour of exclusion?"

Corso raised his eyes to Monica, who was standing in front of the desk. He found her smile both beautiful and insufferable.

"There are regulations," he began, for want of anything else to say.

"In your opinion," she raised her shoulders in the affected manner so characteristic of her, "is saying that Bettini has a dead cat in his head 'an insult-stroke-verbal-abuse'?"

The man in the blue jacket and moccasins went towards the door with the teacher of religion. When they had gone, Corso and Monica were alone.

"When I had a crisis," Monica said, "you were the first to know, and you covered for me when I was seeing that other man and substituted for me when I took time off. And you even supported me when I thought I was in love with you. So I have a right to tell you what I think, don't I?

Corso said nothing.

"What happened to you was terrible, of course it was, but that was twenty years ago. It's time to put it behind you and think of your present life."

Corso turned and pondered the world outside the window.

A woman on her way to the supermarket, an old man on a bicycle, two women sweeping the courtyard opposite in front of the primary school. All under the overhead sun of 2.37 p.m.

"There is no present life." The words slipped from his lips.

Monica bent towards him.

"Nonsense. You're a wonderful person." She rested a hand on his forearm. "A brilliant teacher, I know that . . ."

"You know nothing," Corso said with ferocious calm.

Monica withdrew her hand and they remained silent, like boxers each staring from his corner at a different point in the ring and wondering whether it was worth starting again. Then Corso got up, lightly touching her shoulder with a gesture that could have been either absent-minded or apologetic, and went out.

An hour later he was driving along a road that sometimes followed and sometimes crossed the twisting course of a river. The cassette player was playing the Leonard Cohen recording he had taken from its case in the boot.

He said, "I've had a vision and you know I am strong and holy. I must do what I've been told."

Corso had lived with every syllable of that song. Yet, gutted, emptied, turned inside out, pulled to pieces and reassembled, it had remained just what it was: a song. A beautiful song. It had been the same with the letters from Autumnal: the paper, the writing, the fingerprints, the typewriter, the postmarks. All useless. Merely letters that had arrived at regular intervals from different countries, containing the lyrics of a beautiful song. And the war had ended twenty years ago, its outcome carved in stone, Michelle and Martina had been lost, and he was the only person not to have realised that fact.

You poor bugger, he thought.

He stopped the car near a votive statue, changed into his

boots, pulled on his jumper and walked off down a path that disappeared among the larch trees. He did not stop for three hours until he was under a wall that shared the severity of things that have narrowly missed greatness. He looked at the large plaque crossed by two diagonal fissures, and then at the dark clouds that filled the part of the sky from which darkness would come, and started out.

When he reached the top, day and night were fighting their last battle. The plain was already full of lights, and from the clouds which had now taken over the greater part of the sky, came a cold and bruising wind. Round him were few signs of life: just chamois dung, a few stalks and a clump of yarrow with no flowers.

He leaned into space and imagined his body stretched on the rocks below, an arm bent behind his back in an unnatural position. He held on to the image, hoping something in him would rebel against it, but his heart beat no faster and his eyes maintained their steady stare.

He understood now that the last thing still living in him, the hot mass of hate and pride that had kept him breathing, was beginning to fail, and that once it had gone cold nothing would be left of him but the inert semblance of a human being, something resembling yet infinitely distant from the life that had produced him.

For the first time he really believed in the possibility of madness. All he needed was to take one more step forward.

22

"Stick this under your arm."

"There's no need."

"You knocked on the door at six this morning, it's for me to decide what you need."

Corso inserted the thermometer under his jumper and took another sip of tisane. He was sweating all over and his hands seemed out of control, so he put the cup down again at once. The smell of food people had eaten the previous evening turned his stomach.

Cesare had resumed drying glasses from the dishwasher.

"I'll get you some trousers," he said. "They won't be the latest fashion, but at least they'll cover your legs."

Bip.

"And give that to me."

Corso passed him the thermometer. Cesare held it up first to the grey light coming from the window and then under the neon light, before finally putting it down on the bar.

"See for yourself," he said.

Corso lifted the thermometer close to his face and nodded.

"No aspirin till you've had something to eat," Cesare said.

He went upstairs for ten minutes, during which Corso laid his head on his arms at the bar, listening to footsteps, a door squeaking and the Arab music.

Earlier, night had resumed the offensive, sprinkling a fine cold dust from the sky as if someone had been sandpapering a star made of ice. His hands had been stiff, his trousers torn, and he could no longer read the time on his Cyma, so he had built two banks of stones in the lee of the nearest larch to be both his bed and his grave, and here he had huddled to listen to the childlike, comforting sound of the snow.

When he opened his eyes at first light there had been a thin white carpet covering the rocks, as if embroidered with small stitches. Perhaps ermine.

He remembered an animal, long and silent, coming up to him in the dark, sniffing him without fear and going away again, as if he had been no more than a piece of dead wood or a meaningless gesture. An object.

Now he looked up to watch the aspirin dissolving in the glass.

"You should bring your girlfriend here sometime," Cesare said. "Maybe she can stop you trying to kill yourself."

Corso waited for the effervescence to settle. On a plate beside the glass were two slices of bread, ham and a knob of butter, with some scrambled egg.

"Perhaps she should marry someone your age," Corso said, drinking as he spoke.

"That would make sense," Cesare responded with a shrug.

While Corso was eating, the seven o'clock bus passed. There was clearly no-one waiting at the stop, because the driver merely changed gear as if the engine needed to take a deep breath before the hairpin bends. Then the sound vanished. Snow dripped from the roofs.

"There's something new about the wolves," Cesare said. "Want to hear it?"

Corso merely lifted his chin.

"The mountain community has got some dogs from Spain for those who use the alpine pastures in summer. These new dogs spend all day sitting under the trees, it never even enters their heads to show any interest in any animal that runs away from them, but if a wolf comes by they chase it off with its tail between its legs, and if it won't go they're capable of leaving it for dead." He nodded in appreciation of the perfection of this. "All you need do is show them the land they are to guard and they get to work; in other respects they're the same as domestic dogs. You can even let them sleep with children. How about that?"

Corso continued to stare at Cesare's biblical face.

"Great," he said, and looked round for the dog Brian.

"He's upstairs," Cesare said.

"You let him into the house"

"He was the one who wanted that."

"But I thought he wasn't allowed in."

"He wasn't."

"And now he is?"

"Now he is."

The door opened to reveal a slender figure. Outside a full sun was now shining. There was something impatient about these mornings hurrying to turn into afternoons, and of this season hastening towards summer. Corso was aware of this, but didn't know what to make of it.

The newcomer was the forester Corso had met before. "Do you make good coffee for simple peasants?" he said. "Or is that only for the favoured few?"

Cesare filled the filter and hooked it up with a mechanical gesture. The old Faema espresso machine gasped like a cow forced unwillingly to its feet, and coffee the colour of rust began dripping into the cup. Meanwhile the man sat down on the stool next to Corso.

"Much snow up there?"

"Uh-huh," Corso said.

Cesare placed the little cup on the bar. The forester tore the corners off two little envelopes, put them together and carefully slid the contents into his coffee. The arms emerging from his rolled-up sleeves were dark and idle, with a gold bracelet on one wrist.

"I'll take advantage of coming across you to put my mind at rest," he said.

He pulled from his pocket a yellow notepad, put it on the counter and began leafing through it. The cold morning had sharpened the clarity of his blue eyes.

"The Volvo outside is yours, I think?" He read out the registration number.

Corso nodded, playing with a fragment of bread.

The forester sipped his coffee. On his pad were registration numbers and times, the names of villages and of a woman and the sketch of a room or path.

"Yesterday evening someone reported gunshots in the Serra area, where your car was parked. This morning I went up there and found a chamois in some bushes. It had been shot. Obviously hidden by a poacher so he can fetch it when the snow melts."

Corso put the piece of bread he had been playing with in his mouth. The forester finished his coffee and smiled.

"I believe," he said, resting a hand on Corso's shoulder, "that unless those of us who use the mountains help one another . . ."

There was no fuss whatever. Neither cup nor glass was knocked over. Just the short, precise dart of Corso's left hand, which left the forester fighting for breath, his balls gripped in a vice.

"Corso." It was Cesare who spoke.

Corso stared at the open pages of the notepad by the forest-er's cheek.

"Corso!"

Corso looked up at the old man.

"He's got the point."

Corso looked from the man's livid face to the notepad.

"Is it true you've got the point?" Cesare asked the forester.

The man nodded, shuffling the pages of his notepad.

Corso relaxed his grip and the man slid from his stool to huddle winded on the floor.

"I need to use the phone, please," Corso said.

Cesare reached out to activate the payphone.

"Are you going to finish your egg?" he said.

"If I don't, will you give it to Brian?"

"No, it upsets his stomach."

"Then leave it here," Corso said. He stepped over the man with the blue eyes, who had started to cough, and went over to the telephone.

23

"Flying squad."

"Bramard here. I need to speak to Arcadipane."

"The commissario is not free just now."

"It's urgent."

"He can't be disturbed. Please leave a message."

"Who's that? Buozzi? Pedrelli?"

A pause.

"Pedrelli."

"Put me on to Arcadipane."

Silence.

"Hello?"

"Pedrelli, this is Bramard. Put me on to Arcadipane."

"Of course, Commissario."

Sound of the phone being put down. Call redirected to another line.

"Arcadipane."

"Corso here, can you speak?"

"One moment."

Hand over phone. "Bring it to me later." Steps, door opening, office noises, door closing.

"Well, what the hell do you want?"

"I need you to do something for me."

"But what . . . ?"

"I need you to send someone to the Cottolengo."

"Not bloody likely! Last time that nun got up my arse!"

"Since when have you been scared of nuns?"

"That fucking nun! She complained to the Curia, and they got on to the questore, and he called me."

"It's nothing to do with the Pontremoli woman."

"Really? Are you offering yourself as a volunteer?"

"No. I need you to send someone good."

"I've got hundreds of good people sitting around here doing nothing."

"It won't need much."

"Meaning?"

"Half an hour there and maybe a couple of hours in the office, if whoever you send is even half awake."

Sound of a door opening. Hand over the phone. "Yes, yes, later!" Door closing.

Click of a lighter, followed by a long puff.

"O.K., make me laugh, go on, I've been bored to death all day."

24

That morning Jean-Claude Monticelli woke early, showered, ate a big breakfast and took a taxi to the airport, from where he caught a flight to Zurich at 11.45.

The Swiss customs forced him to wait for gun control, killing time with magazines and Americano coffee, which was served free in the airport business lounge. Finally the customs official had thrust his florid peasant face into the room and said: "Sorry to keep you waiting, Signor Monticelli, everything's fine as usual."

The car waiting for him in the airport's covered car park had a windscreen covered in pollen from a plant that had flowered early because the season was so unusually far advanced. This made even the Prussian-blue coachwork seem opaque and dead. So he stopped at a service station to have the car washed and waxed, arriving at Locarno half an hour later than planned.

Reaching the house a few minutes after five, he opened the door to a carpet of envelopes and advertising leaflets, a lot of post after only six days' absence.

He pushed it all aside with his foot, parked his bags and rifles in the entrance hall, and went into the kitchen to turn on the kettle and get the teapot ready.

While the water was heating he went up to his room, had a second shower, changed into loose clothes made of raw cotton and took a package wrapped in cloth from the bedside table. Then he went down to the next floor, filled the teapot, and went out onto the terrace to sit in front of the lake in a chaise longue.

A pair of swans were swimming not far from the landing stage where his six-metre boat was moored. Now and then they turned their heads towards one another like periscopes as they chattered. They seemed not to be going anywhere in particular, just moving around. The only boat out at that moment was motionless in the middle of the mirror of water; it belonged to a neighbour from across the lake who had made a fortune from air conditioning in China.

Monticelli poured himself tea and unwrapped the cloth, letting the horizontal light of the setting sun shine on the opaque black of the pistol. It was a versatile weapon, Italian, with a good kick, designed to make the least possible noise. He looked at it with a distracted air, opening the barrel, checking that it contained only one bullet and, having spun it round, closing it again with a snap.

A sound from the house summoned him.

He crossed the living room, with its practical teak furniture, largely monochrome apart from a bookcase made of red sheet-metal from a container, and sat down at the large desk.

He took a small video camera out of a drawer, fastened it above a screen, and pressed a key to wake his P.C.

"I'd no idea you were back," said a girl, smiling as she emerged from the darkness of the screen. "I did try."

"It was a good attempt," Monticelli said. "I wanted to hear your voice."

The girl, about twenty years old, nodded to show she had also wanted contact with him.

"Well?" she said, forcing herself to pout. "How many did you kill, then?"

Jean-Claude pretended the matter needed thought.

"One," he held up one finger.

"Female or male?"

"A beautiful male, nine years old, a hundred and forty kilos."

"Bad boy!" The girl laughed.

Her eyes were a luminous grey; her hair dark brown and short without seeming short. Her very fair skin had been marked by the sun with freckles, the outline of dark glasses and the bright pink of a burnt nose.

"What are you busy with today?" Monticelli asked her.

"Apart from fighting dysentery? We're going into a nearby village to try and get them to join the programme. D'you think we'll succeed?"

"Will you be talking or just listening?"

"I carry water, take notes, swat flies and have dysentery. Quite enough to do for an apprentice."

"But are you happy?"

"Madly. It's fantastic here. I mean, it's terrible but fantastic at the same time. The others are fantastic too. Philip, Sheila, Marco, all of them. D'you know who the only surly one is? A Swiss called Pieter!"

They both laughed.

"I have to go now. We apprentices can never let ourselves be late. I'll call you late this evening, if that doesn't disturb you, we'll be able to talk a bit then."

"Why should I be disturbed?"

"You might have someone there with you."

"Let's talk this evening."

"O.K., kiss you, then."

"Kiss you, Clémentine."

Turning off the computer, Monticelli went back to the terrace to sip his tea and watch the lake rippling slightly in a breeze from the valley. When the teapot was empty, he took the pistol from the table, put the barrel against his temple and pressed the trigger.

The bolt snapped shut on the empty gun. The swans, still circulating round the pier, heard it and swerved towards the centre of the lake without hurrying.

Jean-Claude put down the pistol to drink the last drop of tea in the cup. Then he pulled an alpaca rug over his legs and fell asleep.

25

Corso sat down on one of the four chairs round the table. Buozzi had been the one to take him down and ask him to have a seat. Arcadipane was "on his way back" from a meeting at Headquarters, and would be with him in a few minutes.

It was not difficult to guess that this room was used for interrogations: no windows or superfluous furniture, sound-proof walls, the usual large mirror and artificial light. The walls had been recently painted a pale green and the floor was grey rubber.

At one time this basement had been used for filing and the interrogation room had been on the top floor, and in his own police days, Corso used to be able to seat those he was interrogating with their backs to the window, so that he could listen while at the same time looking at the spire of the Mole Antonelliana visible behind the R.A.I. auditorium without seeming to be completely uninterested in what he was hearing.

It was perhaps for this reason that he could not remember any of those faces now. He had never looked at them, but remembered well the stone roof and the spire being pelted with storms, covered in snow, white in sunlight, or shining in the dull rains of autumn, and barely visible at all in thick early-morning fog.

A girl came into the room. He realised he had caught sight of her briefly once a few weeks before, with a small twisted spoon in her ear, apparently sunk in a sea of troubles.

Ignoring him, she now sat down at the far end of the table, took a small computer out of her bag and switched it on. When she sat down, Corso noticed a faint trace of petrol in the air, and when the screen lit up her face he noticed a small stud, possibly amber, set in the olive skin of her right nostril. She was wearing a khaki shirt under a leather jacket, with black jeans and heavy carapace-green boots only partly laced up.

"Are you a vegetarian?" she asked.

She had a slow, very feminine voice, despite her appearance and age.

"No," Corso said. "And you?"

The girl shrugged. "Not in the least."

The wrists emerging from her jacket sleeves resembled the joints of an ancient draughtsman's lamp. But her slimness gave no hint of illness, fragility or deprivation. Corso guessed she was probably about twenty-five.

"Who sent you here?" he said.

The girl tapped a couple of computer keys. She had five fingernails bound up with adhesive tape.

"The boss."

"Who is your boss?"

She took a dozen notebooks out of her bag.

"Not you," she said, piling them beside her computer.

Corso looked more closely. In fact, there were only three notebooks; the others being small pads, except the two that were just pieces of paper held together with string.

When the girl came into the room he decided it was only 10 per cent likely that she had come there deliberately, 30 per cent that she had been shown into the wrong room by mistake, and 60 per cent that Arcadipane had sent her because he wanted Corso's opinion on some other case. Now the 10 per cent had become 90, and it was not worth asking himself what the remaining 10 per cent might be.

"If you could stop staring at me you'd do me a favour," she said.

Her cheekbones were Nordic despite her black hair, while her light, strong shoulders suggested Balkan origin. Her nose and mouth were entirely French. In fact, any description of her could have ended with "despite the fact that . . .", thus creating an absolute need to go on staring at her.

"Are you a police officer?" Corso said.

Her frank eyes looked over the screen at him for the first time, as if about to leap at him, but at that moment the door opened to admit Arcadipane, followed by the usual cloud of smoke.

The commissario sat down and fought for breath, his jacket crushed from sitting in his car. The smoke immediately settled under the ceiling.

"Let's get one thing clear," he started, his cheeks sinking as he drew in one final mouthful of smoke. "This meeting never happened, I never asked Isa to do anything, nor has anything ever been suggested to me by any depressed former commissario that I only meet occasionally for old times' sake, O.K.?"

No-one spoke.

"Well, then." He squashed the remains of his cigarette on the floor with the toe of his shoe. "Isa has been to the Cottolengo to talk to that bloody nun and, God knows how, she got permission to take away your scribbling friend's notebooks. I've asked her to check the car registration numbers the dotty woman recorded on December 24 during the last seven years and compare them. Assuming that what the woman wrote makes any sense at all . . ."

The girl continued to stare at the screen without making

the slightest effort to conceal her boredom. When she linked her hands behind her chair, the straps of her holster outlined larger breasts than her otherwise slender figure had led him to expect.

"... in my opinion it's all a waste of time, because there's no earthly reason why Autumnal should have come by car and parked in that particular street. However, since you promised this was the last favour you would ask of me ..."

In the silence that followed, Arcadipane realised that no-one other than him had felt a need for any recapitulation. Taking his cigarettes from his pocket, he immediately stuck one between his lips.

"Let's pull this tooth, then," he said, lighting the cigarette.

The girl detached her back from the chair and turned the computer with one finger so they could both see the screen. It showed two circles divided into coloured segments.

She pointed at the first circle, "These registration numbers occurred more than once in the seven years. There are nineteen of them among the two hundred and eleven recorded in the notebooks. The second diagram is a breakdown of the nineteen: six belong to people who are or have been working on the site, eight others are local residents, and four belong to people who had or still have a relative resident at the Cottolengo. The last one" – she indicated the smallest slice of the cake with one of her taped fingers – "turned up three times in the seven years. The car belongs to a certain Amedeo Luda."

She looked at the two men without enthusiasm, turned the computer back towards herself, stretched her legs and once more leaned back in her chair.

"Who is this Amedeo Luda?" Corso said.

The girl dropped her chin onto her chest.

"No-one asked me anything about that," she said, barely

glancing at Arcadipane. "You told me not to piss outside the pot, right?"

"I also told you to show proper respect for your superiors," the commissario said. "Have you or have you not checked up on this Luda?"

The girl turned back to her monitor.

"He's eighty-three years old, of aristocratic origin, a widower who lives in the hills. He used to be a shareholder in a bank and sat on various committees, but he's best known as a collector of Japanese art. About a hundred metres from the Cottolengo there's an antique dealer highly respected as an expert on oriental art. He's friends with this Luda, and it seems Luda always goes to see him at that time of year to buy something to give as a Christmas present."

"How do you know that?"

"I made a phone call."

"Who to?"

"The shop," said the girl. "I said I wanted to buy something, and was trying to find out which dealer had sold a piece that a collector gave to my father last Christmas. The shopkeeper asked if the collector was Luda. I said yes. So he . . ."

"Alright, alright, we've got the point. This is not a competition to see who can make the longest speech. Anything else?"

The girl pushed aside the lock of hair covering one side of her face. On the right of her neck, the side where her head had not been shaved and her hair was shoulder-length, she had five little signs tattooed in blue, perhaps the Pleiades. The spoon was in her left ear.

"No," she said.

"And you?" Arcadipane asked Corso.

"No."

"O.K., you can go now."

The girl closed her computer.

"What about these notebooks?"

"What did the nun tell you?"

"To take them back."

"Then that's what you'll do."

The girl threw the notebooks casually into her bag together with the computer, and stood up. She was a little over one metre seventy, but so thin as to look taller. On the point of opening the door, she turned.

"When do I get to go out again?"

Arcadipane did not look at her.

"When you learn to address your superiors appropriately and keep your hands to yourself."

"Meaning?"

Arcadipane stubbed out his cigarette on the floor near the first one to indicate there was no more to be said, and the girl went out.

The two men remained in silence for a second which lengthened into a minute. But Arcadipane had something to do upstairs and did not enjoy smoking in rooms without windows.

"I don't think the octogenarian Luda is the grizzled fifty year-old we're looking for," he said.

"Probably not." Corso scratched a hand. "But what would you do if this case were not twenty years old?"

Arcadipane lit yet another cigarette and gave a long meditative series of pulls at it, turning the packet repeatedly on the table: first horizontally, then vertically, then horizontally again.

"Let's make a pact."

"What?"

"You take the girl with you."

Corso looked at the empty chair where she had just been sitting.

"Half the men upstairs want to screw her and the other half hate her guts," Arcadipane said. "Or both. Not that she goes out of her way to encourage them. Maybe she's a lesbian, I don't know, I don't understand these things. But in any case she needs a dose of reality. I expect you see her type every day in your school."

"Why is she in disgrace?"

Arcadipane traced a couple of circles in the air with his cigarette, as if to indicate a combination of things.

"She's impudent, arrogant and foul-mouthed. And then a couple of weeks ago she broke a colleague's nose."

"Why?"

"She says he made a pass at her."

"And did he?"

"How the devil would I know? You've done my job, haven't you? It's not as if I run a confessional, where all can come and confess their sins."

"Transfer her, then."

Arcadipane shook his head.

"With all these idiots I have on my hands, when one finally arrives with real talent, you expect me to get rid of her? I'd be a bloody fool if I did." He stretched out a leg to crush the cigarette-end he had let fall to the floor. "On top of that she's Mancini's daughter."

"Mancini . . . ?"

"Mancini, Mancini." Arcadipane nodded. "If it had been any other Mancini, would I have said she was Mancini's daughter?" He rummaged in the packet for another cigarette. "Well, will you take her on?"

26

It was a short journey; about fifteen minutes to get out of the centre, pass the bridge, climb the first hairpin bends and arrive above the city. Below lay the river, the piazza and the main streets, where the occasional glitter of sun on a windscreen was the only live thing. *The distant pounding of scales in the sea . . .* thought Corso. The girl had been staring at her mobile phone ever since they got into the car, and now it gave a signal.

"Turn here," she said.

Five hundred metres of level road with art nouveau villas, elder trees and expensive-looking gardens, and they found themselves in a small clearing in front of No. 12, where the road accessible to cars ended.

They got out, leaving the engine of the Polar running.

There was a simple wrought-iron gate with old stone pillars. On the right was the family's name and on the left a heraldic shield with a unicorn surrounded by ivy. Beyond the gate, the drive continued gently upwards through an elegant garden with a few tall trees, hedges and other low plants, as far as the villa, which stood self-confident but modest at the top of the rise.

Isa rang the bell on the gate. The sun was lighting the clearing, shaded by the trees growing nearest the fence. The heat made it difficult for drops of resin that fell on the asphalt to solidify.

"Yes?" said a woman's voice.

"We are looking for Signor Luda."

"Who shall I say it is?"

"Police."

No comment from the intercom.

Isa, who had left her jacket in the car and was not wearing her holster, stepped back so that any C.C.T.V. image would include Corso, who was a couple of steps behind her.

"One moment." Then the sound of the receiver being replaced.

"The fucking cow!" Isa said.

Corso took a firmer stance and thrust his hands deep in his pockets.

Hours spent sitting on the stairs waiting for Forensics, night-time ambushes and afternoons motionless in front of the type-writer waiting for a report, a commission, a telephone call or a flash of inspiration, this was what he missed about police work. Time inevitably spent in boredom, assembling and reassembling the pieces of a jigsaw.

He contemplated the garden beyond the bars. Apart from some maple trees and a magnolia, he recognised none of the plants. But they had clearly been carefully selected to hide the house from view at all times of year. A deliberate design that avoided the facile temptations of both order and chaos. An equi-librium supplementing that of the villa and its backdrop of mountains, just visible in the heat-haze.

He turned to the girl, who passed a hand across her brow as though troubled by an insect.

"That really screwed me up!"

Corso watched her go back to the car, search in her jacket and return firmly to the gate. She was holding her police identi-fication badge up for the camera with her other hand on the intercom, when the right-hand side of the gate began to open.

"Put that badge away," Corso said. "It isn't necessary."

They proceeded more slowly up the last part of the drive, where the asphalt gave way to cream-coloured cobbles, each the size of an egg yoke. Several details on the house conflicted with its art nouveau style: a Doric column, a mullioned window with two lights, a few Gothic windows, a medieval stone fountain and a Romantic architrave over the door of what may have been a garage. On the side where the hill sloped down among the trees, Corso made out a small wooden temple in oriental style.

Luda was waiting for them under the portico, a few steps from where they had left the car. The loose skin of his face, his emerald cardigan, his exotically wide trousers and abundant white hair gave the impression of a man who had won a generally favourable compromise with time.

He introduced himself: "Amedeo Luda." Only his hands and his physique betrayed his eighty-three years.

"I'm Corso Bramard, and this" – Corso indicated Isa – "is Police Officer Mancini."

Isa and the man exchanged glances, the man with gentle indifference, Isa with her hands thrust into her tight pockets. What had seemed a singlet was in fact a shirt with its sleeves cut off.

"We'd like to ask you a few questions," Corso said, turning to look at the road they had come by. "It won't take very long."

"Of course," the man said. "Would you like to walk in the garden or shall we go into the house?"

"The house will be fine."

The man led them along an arcade at the end of which an open door gave onto a corridor with small pictures of flowers and bamboo. Low terracotta statues stood like guards on either side. The floor was wood and a room at the far end was warmly lit by a large window.

"I wonder if I may go so far as to ask you to be good enough to take off your shoes," the man said, exchanging his own clogs for some slippers lying just inside the entrance. "I know it's a bore," he smiled, "but at my age people can have worse obsessions."

Corso used his left foot to push off his right sandal and his right foot to push off his left, then, selecting a pair of slippers from the shelves by the door, he made a sign to Isa. Six more pairs remained, arranged in order of decreasing size.

"If the young lady would rather not," Luda said from the middle of the corridor, "then no matter. Hospitality is the elder sister of regulation, and the more reasonable of the two."

They joined him in the main room, where walls decorated in antique green were hung with delicate panoramas and a few erotic prints. To the south the large window overlooked a terrace crowded with potted plants.

"Can I tempt you to some tea?" Amedeo Luda said. "Our Ester makes a delicious blend."

Corso shook his head to say no for both of them. Luda sat down on the sofa and prepared to listen. His composed expression, light-brown face and feminine lips gave him the look of a serene monk.

"Have you known Domenico Tabasso long?"

"All his life," Luda said. "His father Gianni and I were friends in our university days. I was in the hospital corridor when Domenico was born."

Corso ran his eyes over several raku bowls on a low table and a reading-stand with an open book. He read the autograph on the first page.

"That was one of the most extraordinary meetings of my

life," Luda said. "The man seemed very shy, almost impossibly so, but someone at the embassy granted us an audience. Unlike me, Gianni could speak excellent Japanese and when Mishima realised that he became very friendly."

Corso moved further along the wall. On a bureau was a cup with opaque green reflections.

"An extremely unusual variety of jade," Luda said. "Only ever worked during the early seventeenth century. Do you have an interest in oriental art?"

"Sadly, no," Corso said, his eyes moving to the part of the room behind their host. "Do you often see Domenico Tabasso?"

"Not so often since Gianni died, but he rings me up now and then for advice."

"And when that happens you go and see him?"

"Nearly always. There's no sense in moving such delicate pieces about unless you have to."

"Naturally," Corso agreed.

A dozen photographs were propped on the marble mantelpiece. Among them, in black and white, a portrait of a woman in early twentieth-century clothes who was probably Luda's mother, and a man on horseback in the uniform of the Royal Italian Cavalry. Snapshots, in the faded shades of the seventies showed meetings of friends, the conferment of an honour, a tennis court, and Luda himself as a young man on the steps of a temple with two women in traditional dress.

Corso turned to look at the man's back and the fluffy white hair that hid the collar of his cardigan, then looked for Isa. She was leaning against the doorpost muttering into her mobile phone. He stared at her until she looked up, then indicated the photos on the mantelpiece with his chin before taking several steps in the direction of the window. A large Buddha in worn lacquer was guarding the door.

"Do you often spend Christmas Eve in Tabasso's shop?" he asked, sniffing the light air coming in through the slightly open French window.

Luda turned, the same gentle expression on his face.

"To buy something as a last-minute present for friends," he said. "A habit of mine ever since Gianni first started the shop. The orient has taught me that traditions are vital for peace of mind, wouldn't you agree?"

Corso nodded, staring at the layer of dust above the city. It was a good city, if the truth be told: keen, civilised and in no way uncaring, but also dirty, with a ferocious streak. You needed a certain dose of disillusion and patience to understand it, and it continued to deceive many. Especially the ingenuous, the lazy and the impatient. In other words, most people. But no-one at present in that room: Luda because he was too old, Corso because he had built his career on understanding Turin, and the girl because she combined in herself the city's essential features: contrition, craziness, a sense of duty, genius, geometry and a certain shame for which one is never to blame but does everything possible to conceal.

"I'm afraid we've been wasting your time for nothing," Corso told Luda. "There have been robberies in the area and we've had to check the registration numbers of cars. A waste of time, but an unavoidable formality. May I go outside?"

"Of course." Luda got up to give him room to pass.

On the terrace, in the damp and sticky shade cast by the potted plants, there were no chairs or tables. The unshaded sun, wherever it could, had faded a floor made of hexagonal tiles coloured grey, garnet and black that must originally have come from some apartment.

Corso went to the parapet where Luda joined him. They studied the green downward slope of the hillside punctuated by red roofs, the white cupola of the Gran Madre church, the river and, beyond the great piazza, an intricate network of streets.

"When I was a boy," Luda said, indicating the river and the cars lined up along it, "from June onwards we would see the sands crowded with umbrellas and bathers. There were so few cars that you could hear people's voices from here. But you are too young to have known Turin in those days. I'd guess you're from Cuneo, or am I wrong?"

Corso took a sucai lozenge from his pocket and put it in his mouth. It was warm and offered little resistance. Not what he had hoped for, but ultimately just what he should have expected.

"Roero," he said.

Luda nodded. Now, in full sunlight, the subtle network of his wrinkles was fully revealed. Corso thought he could detect a trace of powder at the base of the old man's ear.

"At the beginning of the century," Luda said, his elegantly ancient hands on the parapet, a great-aunt of mine married a Revel, but they had no children and that branch of the family died out. Do they still own all those farms around Palormo?"

"Quite a number."

"A splendid area, rich earth, undervalued. I've always preferred that to the Langa."

Corso looked down at the garden below them, where a wooden gangway passed between islands of beautifully kept white sand and a few plants. The largest of these had dropped on the ground a circle of intact flowers of an intense lilac.

"Now we'll leave you in peace," he said, dividing the lozenge in two inside his mouth. "We've wasted far too much of your time."

27

"There's a strike today," the fat woman who caught 47B with her each morning had said, adding, "No point in waiting," before turning and walking away in her mock fox-fur collar with the packets of detergent she took for her work cleaning in the city centre. "Turn round and go home again!"

Alone now in the bus shelter she had spent a long time thinking. The darkness had only just lifted. It was very cold. The city was a single huge noise of cars. The sky was overcast.

She could go back to the block of flats with its green tiles where she lived, ring the bell, wait for her mother to find the energy to get out of bed, then climb the stairs, dump her back-pack, switch on the T.V. and pass the morning on the sofa, with an occasional glance towards the room where her mother had gone back to bed with the blinds pulled down and the medicines on her bedside table. Or she could wait in the bar on the ground floor with its one-armed bandits until her usual time for coming home. This was what she usually did when there was a strike or she did not feel like going to school.

But that day, without knowing when or why she came to this decision, she found herself walking along the roads she had never previously seen except through the windows of the 47B. Then she did the same thing the next day, and every day after that, all through that winter, the year when she was between eight and nine years old, waking an hour before dawn to cover the streets at a quick walk, wrapped in the windcheater passed down from her cousin, always being late for school nevertheless, since the school was on the other side of the city, near the park and the river and the flat where they had been living before her father for some unknown reason was found dead in Medina.

The women who were her teachers had attributed her behaviour to what was happening at home, to the social services being so slow to take any notice, and to her not having a bus pass. That suited her fine. She would never have admitted that the real reason was that she loved the wonderful smell of her own body after the long hurried walk. A personal smell that made nonsense of the looks the teachers gave her, of the sniggers of her classmates, of the green tiles and her mother's medicines at home, of having to do gym in jeans, and the fact that there was one thing no-one could bring themselves to tell her.

The first person to notice the smell had been the boy brilliant at maths and bad at everything else who sat next her in class. Then others, even the teachers, had mercifully stopped disturbing her when she did not want to be disturbed – which was always.

By the end of the winter she no longer needed to walk across the city because her smell had become permanent to her. So she had gone back to taking the 47B and no-one had wondered why.

"Have those photos you took come out?"

Isa looked at the man beside her, his face covered half by his beard and half by his hair, which was neither curly nor straight. She had noticed the smell of his skin the moment she came into the interview room. A complex and restful smell, like something so old there is no point in asking how old it is. Though he did not live in the city he smelt of wet pavements. Though he did not smoke he smelt of tobacco as if he had a stock of it under his skin that must be absorbed. He also smelt of dog, and there was a dog-like quality about his voice too: dog – dog – dog.

"Why didn't you ask Luda about that woman at the Cottolengo?" she said.

Turning into the service road, Corso pulled up in the shade of the first available plane tree, a few metres from the bridge beneath which the river seemed to be flowing the wrong way.

"No point in asking about things I don't already know. The photos?"

Isa took the laptop from her bag and connected it to her mobile phone, waited for it to find the external source, then began running the pictures she had taken of Luda's mantelpiece.

"This is the one," Corso said.

He got out of the car and came back from the boot with a yellow envelope from which he took several large prints.

"Here's the Pontremoli woman on the day they found her," he said.

Isa compared this to a photograph on her screen that showed a dozen people posing in the garden of a large country house in front of a table from which they had eaten lunch and a swing. With one of her taped fingers she touched the face of a girl sitting on the ground with her legs crossed.

"Is that her?"

"I think so, at sixteen or seventeen."

"And this looks like Luda."

Corso nodded. "The Pontremoli parents are probably also in the picture."

"They must have been quite close friends if Luda keeps a picture of them on his mantelpiece."

"There are a dozen people here; his closest friends could have been others."

"That would explain why Luda has never been to see the

Pontremoli woman, even though his friend the antique dealer is so close to the Cottolengo."

Corso thought about this, staring at the highly polished steering wheel of the Polar.

"He might have gone there in the past. The registers only cover the last seven years. However at the moment that means nothing."

"If at the moment it means nothing, what the fuck are we talking about?"

Corso put the photograph back in the folder.

"Do you think you can find out?"

"What?"

"Who the others in that photo are."

Isa looked out of the window of the car. She hated this district, the bar over the road where in an hour or so people would be crowding in for an aperitif, and the lady with the miniature pinscher just getting into a taxi at the crossroads. Left to herself, Isa would have strangled that dog with a shoelace and thrown it into the river. She rested her hand on her stomach.

"I'm forced to do any fucking thing you ask me or Arcadipane won't let me have my gun back. Do you use email?"

"No."

"Do you have a computer? Or a mobile?"

A dark green car stopped a few metres ahead of them. Its driver lit a cigarette. Corso pulled a portable cordless phone from his pocket.

"Good God!" the girl said. "What the fuck can you do with that?"

"Not much."

"Put it away before it gives you lockjaw. Where can I reach you when I've found something?"

Corso gave her his postal address, then took out of his wallet the piece of paper on which he had written the number of his mobile phone. Isa was just inserting the number into her iPhone, when it rang. Corso read ELI on the caller display.

"Oh," said Isa into her phone. "No, I can't now." Pause. "Do what the hell you like. I don't give a fuck."

She hung up, switched off the computer and opened her bag to put it away.

"Tell me what you know about Autumnal." Corso said.

"I know he killed women," Isa said without stopping what she was doing, "cut patterns on their backs and made sure they were found with their blood drained off. After the third one they put you on the case, but while you were working on it and not finding out a single fucking thing, he murdered two more and then your wife and daughter as well. You went to pieces and started to drink and do hard drugs, then tried to arrest one of the vice squad and left the police just in time before they could throw you out.

"I never did hard drugs."

Isa raised her shoulders, indifferent.

"Then you worked for a few months as a private detective for a large company, but continued to drink. In the end a friend helped get you off the booze, and once dried out you went back to your old family home in the hills. You used your old university degree to get a job in a school, where for ten years now you've been teaching eight hours a week, and recently you've started struggling on again in other respects. No particular friends or close relationships. Just one uncle. Income about seven hundred euros a month. No women. You've been known to play cards in a bar now and then. You don't drink much now. Officially no guns, and it seems you've never tried to get hold of one."

Corso stared at her.

"You've given hell to the social services, haven't you?" Isa scratched her nose. "All in all, a fine record."

"That was thirty years ago."

"So what, once you've fucked yourself up you carry the mark of it for the rest of your life?"

"And what about you?"

"What about me?"

Isa took her bomber jacket from the back seat, pushed it into her bag with the laptop, closed the zip and weighed the whole thing as if it were a product sold by the kilo.

"I'm better with computers than the others," she said, stretching her legs and slipping her iPhone into her jeans pocket. "I'll get out here. Call you this evening. Not a guy who goes to bed early, are you?"

"I have an insomnia problem."

"Then we have at least one thing in common."

Corso watched her striding away on long young legs, her gait as confident, flexible and fluent as that of a Slav soldier. Moving off again he reached the crossroads. The traffic passing on the main road was heavy enough to make the Polar vibrate. The lights went green, but as he lifted the clutch there was a knock on the side window. Isa's face was a few centimetres from his own. He lowered the window.

"Was my father really in the shit with the service, like they say?"

Corso felt a craving to smoke. His fingertips remembered the elegance of Gitanes, their perfect uniform white cylinders, and the tenacity of the ash clinging to the tobacco.

"Those were very complicated times," he said.

Isa looked at him, stuck up a finger at the driver behind who had ventured a timid touch on his horn, and disappeared.

28

"Signor Monticelli, the doctor is ready to see you."

Jean-Claude Monticelli put down the magazine, picked up his overnight case and got up from the comfortable armchair where he had just sat down, crossed the room with its burl-wood panelling, smiled at the young secretary who had replaced Renata when she had retired a couple of years earlier with her husband to their house in Majorca, and went into the surgery.

He had always thought Klaus modest, almost shabby, considering the high fees he charged and his unarguable taste for beautiful things, especially if they were blonde or capable of moving at more than 250 kilometres an hour. However, he thought there must be some reason for this: any reminder of the transitory nature of life could not but be contemplated with a measure of bleakness.

He sat down on the cheap plastic chair facing Klaus' elegant desk and smiled. Klaus did not like his patients to bring in other people. Parents, spouses, children – they all had to stay in the waiting room. That was why there was only one chair in front of the desk. And no pictures or certificates on the walls. No distractions.

"Here we are," Klaus said.

A casual glance might have registered a Rembrandt with a paunch and the head of an ox with hair a slightly less violent red than his beard. There was a very lively-looking wart on one cheek. A closer examination would have added a snub nose, pierced ears without earrings, and hands a couple of sizes smaller than one would have expected.

"Here we are," echoed Monticelli, settling his case on his knee. "Have you got everything?"

The man unclasped his little hands, took a folder from a drawer and placed it in the exact centre of the desk. Its laminated cover carried the surgery's name and logo. The logo had been his own idea, based on his memory of the sign of the tavern by the Rhine where once when he was a child his mother had sent him to fetch his father. It showed a beehive over a nest of snakes. Only four people knew its origin.

"Have a look," he said.

Monticelli took the folder and calmly leafed through its five pages. The room was entirely isolated and the two-storey building it formed part of was in an exclusive, leafy hillside area only five minutes from the centre of town. Quiet, inhabited by people with a genetic inclination to discretion.

"That seems convincing," he said, closing the folder. "But you're the expert. What do you think?"

Klaus lifted his shoulders.

"This type of carcinoma needs little diagnosis and has a very rapid course. It is also compatible with your medical history and your present apparent good health and likelihood of death within a few months. I don't need to tell you that anyone who based their diagnosis on a sample of blood or urine would consider it invalid."

"Perhaps because it really is invalid?"

Klaus smiled, revealing a gold tooth. An old story.

"I suppose I shouldn't ask how that could benefit you."

"Do you want to?"

"No, but I wouldn't like to get in the way. Not even with people I've asked to do what I've asked them to do."

Monticelli took a boiled sweet from a transparent bowl on the desk. He unwrapped it, put it into his mouth and rolled the paper until he had made it into a big acacia thorn.

"How long have we known each other?" he said, placing the wrapper on the desk like the needle of a compass pointing to the east.

"Twenty years ago you paid me for a fake diagnosis."

"Have you ever known why?"

"No."

"Has anyone ever come to find out?"

"No."

And we have remained excellent friends these twenty years."

"Excellent."

Monticelli opened his arms and held them suspended, until the man smiled again, more widely this time, revealing a second gold tooth.

"Shall we drink to it?"

"Later," Monticelli said.

He snapped open the locks of his case, searched inside it and placed three white envelopes on the desk.

The man who looked like Rembrandt opened them and quickly counted the money.

"Absolutely correct," he said.

Monticelli nodded while leafing through the diary he had taken from his pocket. Reaching the page he was looking for, he drew a line through the second item on the list, then admired the neat clarity of the pencil line he had drawn.

29

"The photo was taken towards the mid-seventies, but we can't be more exact from this copy. The two lying down are Clara Pontremoli and her brother Gregorio, who was three years older than her. The third child, the very small boy, I don't know. He could be the son of the third couple, who I haven't managed to identify. The other two couples are Luda and his wife, in the centre, and the parents of Gregorio and Clara Pontremoli to the left. It wasn't easy to identify the Ludas, but in the end I found several old photographs in the local press: formal ceremonies, official reunions, a charity dinner. There were plenty of shots of the Pontremolis, since the papers mentioned the mother's suicide, the son's accident in Greece and the father's heart attack"

Silence at the other end of the phone, apart from the background music of fingers tapping on a keyboard. Not real music, Corso thought.

"The father, Bartolomeo Pontremoli, worked in real estate all his life, first in a firm under his own name and later as a consultant. There were big investments; he made money from the expansion of Turin in the sixties and seventies but came from a rich family in any case. He made friends impartially with priests, Christian Democrats and communists, but he was not officially affiliated anywhere. There was nothing shady about his professional or personal C.V. He financed and was a partner in two bookshops, one antiquarian in the city centre, the other scientific. Some charity work. Committee member of several cultural associations. His obituary describes him as 'one of the first to introduce Turin to contemporary Japanese art in the sixties following his many visits to the Orient'. This probably accounts for his connection with Luda, because they were never fellow students: Luda studied Law, while Pontremoli took a degree in Economics immediately after the war. His wife on the other hand" – more tapping on the keyboard – "was Beatrice Gallizio. They were married in '52, she being about ten years younger than him, of good family, a qualified teacher who began university studies but did not finish them. Their son Gregorio was born in '54 and Clara in '57. She had never had to work for a living, and never recovered from the attack on her daughter, which led to depression treated with medication and several weeks in hospital, and finally the dive from the balcony. Second floor only, but it was enough. There seems to be a report on paper of the summons and presence of the Carabinieri, but that's all; it was never computerised. You were connected with the case at that time, weren't you? Didn't you know about it?"

"I did."

"Then two years later their son Gregorio kicked the bucket. Car accident in Greece, where he was on a study trip: he was an academic, a Hellenist. A lorry took a curve too wide and knocked him off the road at a place where there was no parapet. His car was smashed on the rocks, end of story. An announcement in the papers, a few photographs. Face like the back of a bus. His father seems to have had him buried in the cemetery of a small Greek island so he could have 'the sea in front of him and his beloved archaeological remains at his back'."

Silence, with something fizzy being poured into a cup and

swallowed, and more music that was not music.

"But not a sausage about the Ludas, apart from what I told you the other day and the announcement of his wife's death in '87 'after a long illness, lovingly cared for by her husband'. The two had no children. I can do nothing about the other, nameless, couple. Or about the third child, the little boy. So there we are, back where we started – in the shit."

Corso detached his back from the wall he'd propped himself against for the whole of Isa's telephone call, and leaned on the windowsill. Fresh night air moved at the window, and, in the distance, the flashes of a storm. Now he could hear Gregorian chanting from the telephone.

"You've done good work," he said. "At least now we know for certain that the Pontremolis and the Ludas knew each other."

"But you said that means nothing, didn't you? In any case I don't give a fuck about any of it, so don't waste your time kissing my arse. I'm only doing what you wanted because the boss is your friend."

Corso moved his head right, left and backwards to loosen his neck then looked at the Autumnal folder lying on the table. Before the telephone rang he had checked the statements again, also the report from Forensics and the photographs of the hut where Pontremoli had been found. She was the key, the woman it had all started with, the only one left alive by Autumnal, the one the hair in the envelope was telling him to go back to.

But what had been her relationship with Autumnal? Lovers?

No-one connected with Clara Pontremoli had ever talked of her as a flirt, or even suggested she had ever fancied anyone. No new acquaintances, no letters or phone calls, hours unaccounted for, or lies: the evidence from the inquest was that Clara Pontremoli's romantic life had been restricted to her fiancé, who during the time of the attack had been under strict supervision, and could never have reached the hut without it being discovered.

And Luda? The man who parked in front of the Cottolengo on the very days Autumnal went to visit Pontremoli. Who had known Clara since she was a girl, being a close friend of her father whose passion for Oriental art he shared. But Luda is too old to be Autumnal.

Corso approached the table to have another look at the photos of the interior of the hut and the leaves that had covered its floor.

"Have you dropped dead?" The telephone receiver spoke again. "Well, what the fuck shall we do?"

"Let's go about it the old way," he said.

"What's that?"

"We'll go and have a word with a tart."

30

He did two hours of lessons, then spent an hour in the library correcting exam scripts, and another walking in the courtyard putting in time till he had to be back in class for the one o'clock lesson. Monica had a free day on Wednesdays, so he spoke to no-one, apart from another colleague who asked him to deal with two particular students during the last hour, since they were persistently absent from her own classes to avoid being questioned. When the bell sounded the end of the school day he waited for the classroom and the corridors to empty, then returned his register to the staff room and went down to the school dining room. He ate without appetite. He was to meet Isa at 3.30 in front of the theatre. He ordered a coffee. The rotating ventilator on the ceiling was squeaking. He hadn't been comfortable reading newspapers for years. The most he could cope with was a bit of radio. He struggled to reach three o'clock.

On his way out to the Polar, he saw the two students smoking by the outside railings with one foot against the wall. When they noticed him they lowered their feet.

"Thanks, Prof," the thinner and more cunning one said. "You've saved our lives!"

Corso opened the door of the car. He felt no sympathy for them, particularly for the thin one, whose cunning was of a cheap variety. The other, he would once have considered stupid. But he was a good boy even if he had only three pairs of trousers that he wore in alternation throughout the year, and if he never made much progress he was also incapable of causing major problems.

"I told her tomorrow you'll be there of your own accord," he said.

"Tomorrow?" said the stupid one in the spiral voice of the stupid.

"What do you have to do today?"

"Nothing," the stupid one said.

"I've got football," said the other.

Corso settled himself behind the steering wheel.

"I told her tomorrow," he said. "Now it's up to you."

The road was empty and he drove fast. The day still warm, but sharp and spring-like. The grain and rye and everything else that the grilling of the last few weeks had forced to grow too fast seemed to have stopped for breath, relying on what was barely a fresh wind, indeed barely a wind at all, and the shade provided by some promising clouds.

Isa was sitting on the pavement waiting. Beside her was a tall, black, aggressive Enduro bike, its tank by no means the original. She had taken off her helmet but not her jacket, and was writing on her iPhone. When she saw him, she slung her bag round her neck, put on her helmet and got into the saddle.

Crossing the railway flyover, Corso passed two traffic lights in close succession, gave a signal and parked. Isa stopped in the shelter of a news stand, chained her helmet to the wheel and frame of the bike and crossed the few metres to the front door where he was waiting.

It was an exceptionally beautiful art nouveau building in only two colours, brick and grey. Its windows were not too pronounced and its façade was concave to match the roundabout formed by the two great royal avenues it faced. There was a lot of traffic, with overhead traffic lights to facilitate it, side roads and the long shadows of late afternoon.

Corso rang one of the bells. The dark clouds had risen a few degrees up the horizon towards the city.

"Madame Gina," he said.

The front door sprang open to reveal a big marble entrance hall. The lift was already in motion, and without a word they set off up the stairs. Isa was wearing the same trousers as the day before, an army shirt, this also with its sleeves cut off, and a rope belt. Her hair was soaked with sweat from the helmet. Corso imagined he could see a small bruise on her neck though there was none.

On the third floor the doors were all alike and nameless, like those on the other floors. Corso rang at the one on the right. Neither of them had yet said a word

Madame Gina opened the door.

"Hello, Bramard," she said. "Nice to see you again."

"Nice to see you, Gina."

"When you phoned I couldn't believe it. Come in."

They went down a corridor to a music room. The fresco-covered ceiling looked weightless and the walls lined with books seemed merely another trompe l'oeil effect by the painter. There was a grand piano in the bow window and four well-upholstered nineteenth-century chairs surrounded a low table like petals round a flower. Nothing else.

"Do sit down."

The order in which they sat down was neither premeditated nor casual.

"You look well," Madame Gina said. "Even a little . . ."

"Older?"

The woman smiled. She shared the face and elegance of Jeanne Moreau. The look of a woman who keeps an arsenal in her cellar but prefers peace and quiet.

"Your girlfriend?"

"A colleague."

"Teacher?"

"Police."

Madame Gina nodded, looking closely at Isa for the first time. An expression redolent of good advice. In any case, the calm of the room and of what was happening in it seemed to have affected the girl, who was sitting quietly, if not exactly composed, staring at the older woman as if into the warmth of a domestic fireplace.

"I've brought a photo from the seventies," Corso said. "I'd like you to identify the people in it."

Madame Gina helped herself to a cigarette from an alabaster box, which was standing on the table like a small animal unwilling to be touched by anyone except its mistress, and lit it. She had stunningly beautiful teeth and was certainly past sixty. Her hands were the hands of someone who had spent a lot of time in the open air when young, and subsequently repaired the damage.

"Tact was never what I admired most in you. Let's have a look."

At a sign from Corso, Isa put the computer on the table and turned it on. Madame Gina took a spectacle case from the pocket of the waistcoat she was wearing over a shirt and skirt that just reached her knees. She perched the glasses on her nose and spent a few seconds looking at the picture.

"Those are the Pontremolis on the left, the Ludas in the middle and the Tabassos on the right. I presume the youngsters will be two Pontremoli children and Domenico Tabasso, who I think would one day inherit his father's antique business. The

Pontremoli son is dead. And you know better than me what happened to the daughter."

The doorbell rang. Madame Gina laid her cigarette on the edge of a large ashtray and got up.

"Excuse me," she said, making her way to the corridor.

They heard the front door of the apartment opening.

"Good afternoon, Amilcare," they heard Madame Gina say. "No, you're not too early at all. How well you look! Oh yes? But when? You've done well. One has to take care of oneself at all costs, at all costs. Joséphine's upstairs. If you'd like to stay for a coffee afterwards, we can chat for a bit. Of course. See you later, my dear."

Gina reappeared, sat down and took up her cigarette, which seemed to have taken care not to burn any lower while it waited for her.

"What sort of people were they?"

"You mean the Pontremolis and the Ludas and so on?"

Corso nodded.

"Rich, cultured and refined, but not people who liked to show off."

"Did you ever have professional dealings with them yourself?"

"Tabasso once or twice, but he was never a regular here or anywhere else. I would say that, on the whole, his marriage was in good order."

"And Luda?"

"Homosexual. Always was. Quite old when he married a good friend of more or less the same age. It suited them both, but she died only a few years later, I think he really suffered then. Of course there were no children."

"Did he have a relationship with either of the other two?"

"No, sex was never a factor in their friendships."

Madame Gina looked at the window, the piano, the books and the other beautiful things around her. She had owned the place for more than forty years. She had not deserved it, or inherited it, or ever searched for it, but she had known how to protect it and preserve it. And enjoy it.

"I had hoped they didn't make those dreadful sandals anymore," she said. "Do you still wear them even in winter with socks?"

Corso continued to keep his eyes firmly on hers; but Gina was no longer looking at him. She stubbed out what was left of her cigarette in the ashtray, then crossed her legs the other way and smoothed down her skirt.

"Your friend is beautiful if rather reserved . . ."

"That's her job."

Two dimples of amusement appeared on Madame Gina's cheeks.

"Yes," she said. "That's what I've always liked in you. You're have the sensitivity of a chick, a sleeping child, rising bread, or a proud boy who has put his underpants on back to front. Sometimes you're even like Chopin when his music tries to move us and succeeds. My Buster Keaton in sandals."

From the corner of his eye, Corso caught the hint of a smile on Isa's lips.

"Ever heard of the Snoring Beauties?" Gina said.

"Never."

"In the early seventies, there was a place in the city where elderly men could spend the night with very young girls who were asleep. The men arrived after the girls had already been put to sleep with a sleeping pill and left before they woke. In this way an old man could caress and enjoy the smell of a young female body, or simply sleep all night beside her without the girl being aware of it and thus able to cause him embarrassment.

Sexual intercourse was not encouraged, indeed it was absolutely forbidden, and the very few men allowed to take part were all distinguished and very carefully selected, and could be relied on to respect the rules. Not a question of money, in fact."

"But?"

"The time came when one of the men didn't respect the rules. A girl fell pregnant. She was underage and there was a risk of scandal but it was hushed up because the men involved were all so well known: politicians, people who flew in from Rome to pass the night, even a few ecclesiastics. The girl's family were probably well paid to keep their mouths shut, or perhaps that wasn't necessary. But in any case, the place was closed down and no more was heard of it."

"Our friends?"

Madame Gina nodded.

"I don't know when they started it, but it was they who ran it till the bubble burst, finding the girls and choosing the men. As I said, it wasn't a question of money, none of them were short of that."

"Beauty?"

"What else? But if I were you I wouldn't stick my nose too much into that business. Reputation is something people don't like to lose even after they're dead."

Corso stroked his beard with one hand, resting the other on his trousers, which were too heavy and too brown.

"I'll go to the bathroom for a moment."

"You know where it is."

Isa glanced at her iPhone, which was vibrating, dropped it back into her bag and took the computer off the table.

"He's a sweet man," Gina said. "Don't you think?"

"Frankly, I don't give a fuck."

"What crude manners!" Gina smiled. "Sweet men are rare,

especially those with principles who act accordingly. Very rare. If you don't learn to recognise that, you'll end up buried under a load of trash. Do you smoke? Help yourself to a cigarette if you like, but I don't usually offer them because menthol is so horrible. Do you know why he left the police?"

Isa shook her head as if saying no to both questions. Madame Gina lit another cigarette, took an exploratory pull, and nodded.

"I'd warned him, the cretin, to leave me in peace, but he must have thought that considering the state he was in, after which . . ."

She took a long pull and smiled and seemed exactly Jeanne Moreau in the film where she stretches out in a bath and starts remembering.

"I had passed the night inside and was not at all in the best of moods, but I enjoyed the whole thing. He was forced to lie face down on the bench, then propped up at the typewriter and made to sign his release, then given a kick in the balls that would have smashed a window. And during all that time not a fly stirred in the office. No-one moved a finger. When he left he handed in his resignation and *voilà!* I believe it was the only time . . ."

"Have you two screwed?"

Madame Gina looked at the girl facing her, about whom she knew nothing but understood nearly everything. Her smile became less confident.

"If you can ask that it proves you don't know him very well. Do you yourself always fall in love so casually?"

"I don't . . ."

Corso appeared at the door.

In the bathroom he had stared a long time at his face in the mirror, trying to work out a link between Pontremoli, Luda, Tabasso and Autumnal. Was the story of the Snoring Beauties connected with the crimes? Could one of the three men be Autumnal? When Gina said don't stick your nose in that business did she mean she didn't want to be involved herself? The possible answers were: "Perhaps, but not as directly as it suits me to think" and "No" or "Yes".

"Gina."

"What, my dear?" She was smiling.

"Has anyone ever asked you about that business?"

"No, I think it's the first time I've spoken of it since I heard about it."

Corso nodded without moving. Isa realised that the visit was over and got up.

"I'll pass by again soon so we can catch up properly," Corso said.

"I hope by then they'll have stopped making those sandals," Gina smiled, raising her hand to wave to him as if he were a child on a merry-go-round and part of her own youth.

31

Domenico Tabasso's shop was in a small recess from the road that ran from the Cottolengo to the old station. Not so much a square or even a clearing, merely an oversight by the mapmaker onto which opened two windows protected by a grille of slender links that protected a shop full of furniture, fabrics, statues and porcelain.

"Wednesday's Closing Day," Isa said, reading the laminated notice on the door.

Corso looked at his watch: 7.12 p.m. He had parked a little distance away and finished his journey on foot, his soles inevitably massaged by the cobbles: a sensation familiar in the older parts of the city. Isa, in contrast, had ridden her bike the whole way, parking on the pavement.

"Shall I look for his home address?"

Corso looked up. He knew that beyond the dome of the church was the closed garden of the Cottolengo, and on the other side of the block the large building that contained the public soup kitchen. Thirty years before, they had gone into that soup kitchen to arrest a man who had killed a child. The man was waiting for them sitting at table, round him the others he shared his meals with every day. He offered no resistance whatever, asking only to be allowed to finish what he had on his plate. But the supervisor said no, so Corso and two other officers had grabbed the man by the coat and carried him outside. It was winter and very cold, and pushing him towards the car Corso had thought: how can evil be so casual?

The man hanged himself in prison three days later. They never discovered why he had strangled the child after taking him from the yard where he had been playing.

"Demand me nothing: what you know, you know: from this time forth I never will speak word."

Isa looked at him.

"What the fuck is that supposed to mean?"

"It's what Iago says when Othello asks him why he has invented so many lies."

Isa looked down the road, which ended in a gentle rise. A young woman with curly hair was looking out from a balcony. Some way further down, a man in a jacket was leaning against the wall and smoking.

"Well, I'm bloody hungry!" she said.

At 8.44 Isa gave Corso his change and handed him a kebab wrapped in tinfoil before sitting down on the steps of the shop to start on her own.

At the nearby kebab house, men were gathered in groups of four or five at little round tables and smoking narghile pipes. The words they were speaking seemed idle, innocuous, almost soporific. Their bodies were slumped on their seats, their eyes hardly moving.

Two boys passed talking and touching arms the way young Arabs often do. They greeted Isa, who responded with a sign as they went to sit with the others.

"This is where I live," Isa said, indicating with her mouth full a seventies block of flats that stuck out among the low houses of the district.

"Why did you never tell me?"

"What the fuck should I have told you?"

"That this was your part of town."

Isa shrugged and went on eating. No cars were moving, but lead they had given off earlier was still stagnant in the air. From time to time domestic sounds of crockery or television reached them above the hum of Arab voices. The smell was that of an exhausted day that had reached its end.

Using his napkin, Corso tried to wipe off the sauce still running onto his hands.

"Were there no Arabs in Turin?"

"When?"

"When you were in the police."

"A few. Why?"

Isa tore off a piece of tinfoil to get at some more bread.

"You look as if you've never eaten a kebab in your life."

Corso stared at the road behind them, with Tabasso's shop, the Cottolengo and Clara Pontremoli, where Luda had parked and Autumnal had signed the registers with a false name. The pieces of the jigsaw nearly fitted, but not quite. He realised he was very tired and longed to be home. He had already spent too many hours in the city. There seemed no point in sitting there with this girl who communicated in four-letter words and happened to be Mancini's daughter.

"Corso. What sort of a fucking name is that," Isa said, cramming the last of her kebab into her mouth "How come they palmed off a name like that on you?"

He watched her take a very long drink.

"Well?"

There was still some beer at the corners of her mouth. And she did indeed have a bruise, and also a small mole above her ear where her head had been shaved, but you could only see it when she turned her head in a certain way.

"My father was in the 'X Mas' partisans. A few days before the end of the war, the communists came to get him and stand him up against a wall. He was saved by his brother, who had supported Badoglio. The two had never talked much and they didn't afterwards either, but my father told his brother he'd like to give him something in return for saving his life. Then my uncle made him promise to let him choose the name of his first child, so when I was born I was called after a friend of my uncle's who had been shot by the Fascists. End of story."

Isa crushed the tinfoil packaging of her kebab and threw it at a nearby litter bin, just missing.

"Bugger that."

Corso crossed to the fountain on the other side of the road for a drink. When he came back, he saw Isa had pulled an envelope out of her bag.

"Here's the report the Carabinieri wrote when Pontremoli's mother threw herself out of the window. Just a few lines and some photos of the balcony and the garden. Nothing much."

Corso took the envelope without opening it.

"How did you get this?"

"A friend owed me a favour."

"Does Arcadipane know?"

"Should I tell him?"

Corso thought for a moment, then shook his head.

"But it might help if you could get something on the story of the Snoring Beauties."

"Where from?"

"Those places where you seem to be able to find everything."

"Do I have your authority for it?"

"I can't authorise you to do anything, but I'll take responsibility for it."

"Fucking hell!" She smiled. "You really are one of the old school."

It was the first time he had seen her smile. Her teeth were beautifully white, if not quite regular, and the corners of her eyes turned slightly down. Her smile compensated for all that was obnoxious in her, though it took time to realise that, simply because it was so obvious. And she did everything to hide the fact that she was beautiful, sad and quite mad.

"For me this is a real bugger, this stuff about old men sleeping with young girls without screwing them. Can you believe it?"

"Yes, because it happened. Have you ever read Kawabata?"

"What's that?"

"He's a Japanese writer."

"You're the literary one," Isa snorted.

"Alright."

"Alright what?"

"Alright, it's late, I have to go home now."

At 10.15 p.m. Isa leaned her bike against a no parking sign and chained it up. Corso waited nearby, contemplating the hideously ugly seven-storey block of flats. The girl looked in her bag for her keys.

"If you're ready to sleep on the couch, we can go and see Tabasso tomorrow morning, which would suit me fine. Just don't get any funny ideas. I'm not Lisbeth Salander, so you needn't think I'll get up in the night, strip naked and come and screw you, O.K.?"

Corso gave her a blank look.

"You've read Stieg Larsson, haven't you?"

"No."

"*The Girl with the Dragon Tattoo?*"

"No."

She touched the stud in her nostril.

"But I think you've got the point."

Corso looked towards the distant silver stain of the floodlit Mole.

"I have to be at school tomorrow morning," he said. "But you go and see Tabasso, just don't mention the Snoring Beauties. Ask him about the friendship between his father, Luda and Pontremoli. See what he can remember about the attack on the Pontremoli girl. He would have been about twenty at the time, and it is something they must have talked about at home."

"O.K."

"Can I keep the report?"

"Yes, it's only a copy."

"Fine."

They looked at each other, then Isa turned to put her key in the lock and vanished.

At 11.54 Corso stopped at the third curve on a little country lane the Polar had struggled to reach. There was nothing in front of him, below him or around him, just the confused shape of several houses on the opposite hill and a light in the window of one of those houses.

Corso stared at it for at least a quarter of an hour over the old motor of the Volvo, listening to Georges Brassens spicing a happy song with fragments of a very sad love.

I've been on my own for twenty years now, he thought.

When Elena turned off her light he put the car into gear and guided its wheels back onto the asphalt.

It was twenty-three minutes after midnight when Corso opened the envelope and arranged the four photographs on the table, together with the one-page typed report signed at the bottom by the Carabinieri officer A neighbour had seen the woman appear on the balcony and climb astride the railing. She had called out to her, someone she had known for years if never as a close friend, but Beatrice Pontremoli, though obviously hearing her, had taken no notice. A moment later she was stretched out on the path in the garden she and her husband had spent so many years caring for. The paramedics who came in the ambulance could only confirm that she was dead. The photos, though of poor quality, showed the balcony from the garden, the path and garden from the balcony, a full view of the garden, and the railing – probably taken from inside the apartment. It was difficult to understand why the pictures had been taken at all.

At 12.45 Corso got up, deciding he had meditated long enough on the report and the photographs, and made him-self a tisane.

At 12.57 he went down into the cellar and began to go through the higher shelves to the right. It did not take him long to find the book because he remembered its spine perfectly. He took it to the uncomfortable armchair in the middle of the room, lit by a standard lamp whose cable ran over the beaten earth of the floor to an industrial socket near the door.

At two minutes past one, for the second time in his life, he opened *The House of the Sleeping Beauties* by Yasunari Kawabata.
    "Don't play tricks in bad taste, and don't even put your fingers into the mouth of a sleeping girl," the woman innkeeper told Old Eguchi.
    Corso took a mouthful of tisane, and read on.

32

The horse was nervous, perhaps it did not want to go into the horsebox again, but the man leading it was ignoring the way it was tugging at the halter, as if he knew its capricious nature only too well and had learnt the best way to deal with it was to pay it no attention. Even so, when he saw Jean-Claude Monticelli, he stopped to give him time to move away from the entrance.

"Good morning, Etienne," Jean-Claude said, moving out of his way.

"Good morning, Jean-Claude."

Once the horse had been settled and the two men found themselves face to face in front of the opening from which the horse was now looking out, Monticelli counted the rosettes on the horsebox door.

"Two more?"

"Yes, a first at Basel and a second at Strasbourg, but they'll be the last, he's getting a bit old for jumping. What saves him is his terrible character, the same thing as saves the rest of us, of course."

They both laughed.

"Shall we get on with what we need to do?" Etienne said.

"Let's do it."

The changing rooms were elegant, bearing no relation to the

conventionally rustic exterior of the rest of the riding school: a floor of Italian stone, lockers with connected electricity, showers, a Turkish bath, a hay sauna, plenty of mirrors, body creams, hair lotions and a nail-care kit.

Jean-Claude sat on a bench to wait while Etienne finished his shower.

He read a couple of messages on his mobile. One was work, the other from Clémentine, ending with one of those little faces she knew annoyed him: a face with its tongue out, in fact. He ignored the work message and answered Clémentine, saying he was well and missed her, and adding something that might make her laugh.

Etienne came in, rubbing his hair with a towel and with another tied round his waist. His body was athletic but not overdeveloped, with shoulders so perfectly proportioned they could have been turned on a lathe. He moved the boots he had dumped with his riding breeches in front of his locker together, and opened the door. Then he sat down astride the bench and held out the documents to Jean-Claude.

"Will you ask me straight out?"

"O.K.," Etienne said, combing back his hair with his fingers. "Are you sure you know what you're doing?"

"Very sure."

"And you're in full possession of all your faculties?"

"Absolutely."

"And is anyone bringing pressure on you to do what you're about to do?"

"Is that a professional question?"

"No, and I've got another question too. Who the devil is this woman? Does Clémentine know she exists?"

Monticelli smiled.

"It's all fine, Etienne. We're all in agreement."

The man, who had been a notary for eighteen years but as a boy had longed to be a vet specialising in large animals, looked at the documents."

"In that case," he said, showing Jean-Claude the first place where he should sign.

It did not take long, five minutes perhaps. Between one signature and the next, while Etienne showed him where to put his initials, Jean-Claude looked out of the window at the race-horses' paddock. He had never cared for horses. He did not like their fearful eyes, nor their nature as the potential victims of predatory beasts that made them tremble at the slightest whisper. He had always believed man must have been hard-pressed when he chose horses for his helpmates for war and travel.

"There, all done!" Etienne said, when the last signature was in place. Then, while Jean-Claude crossed out something in his notebook, he tidied the documents in the folder.

"My compliments," Etienne held out his hand to Jean-Claude. "As of today you're no longer boss."

33

The little girl moved from one side of the play area to the other, thinking about the slides and swings. She was thin, with honey-coloured hair and the big blue eyes of someone who doesn't need blue eyes to look vague and frivolous. The fact was, her legs emerged from moss-green shorts into a rather expensive pair of red sandals, and her arms, like everything else about her, were as rich in harmony as a violin clef.

"Of all the many admirable shadows in this world, I know well which I can compare my little girl to," Corso quoted.

" . . . he thinks of Luda as an excellent customer and an old family friend, that's all. When he took over the business after the death of his father, he says, he went with Luda to China and Japan a couple of times to meet contacts, but after that Luda stopped making long journeys. Health reasons. Since then they have only met or spoken to exchange information. He confirms that Luda's habit of buying presents for Christmas is a tradition that goes back to when his father owned the shop."

Corso shifted the stick of the ice lolly he had just finished. Aniseed. Now the little girl was running over a bridge between two castles. When she got to the end of it she climbed onto a parapet. A woman of about sixty came up and gestured to her to get down. The child went on dangling her legs for a little longer, then climbed down skilfully. There were other children and other nannies, but it was clear that these two were special.

"*Certainly to the foam, to the sea-foam white on the waves . . .*" Corso recited to himself, before reaching out to drop the stick into the litter bin next to the bench.

"What does Tabasso have to say about the Pontremoli woman?"

"He remembers the time she was attacked, they talked about it at home, his parents were friends of the family, but he was about ten years younger than Clara and Gregorio, and says he only saw them regularly till he was about twelve, when they began to spend more time with people their own age and no longer came round with their parents. It seems the photograph we have must have been one of the last to feature all three of them."

"How did he seem to you?"

"Calm, beginning to go bald at the temples. Has a daughter a few months old, and was falling asleep on his feet. If you ask me, he knows fuck all."

Corso stirred the sparse gravel with his right sandal.

"And the Snoring Beauties?"

"No-one has ever heard of them." Isa raised her shoulders. "And there are no documents. As far as I'm concerned it's all just a load of balls, and even if that tart was right, Autumnal would only have been about twenty at the time, so what the fuck could he have had to do with those elderly sods?"

Corso looked at his watch.

"He's late," Isa said.

"'Madame Gina', to you, not 'that tart'," Corso observed.

Isa moved the helmet from her knees to the bench. Her tight shorts came down to just below the knee. Good for gym. Black.

"It was you who called her a tart."

"I know, but you should call her Madame Gina."

"Of course – Madame!"

"Madame Gina."

Arcadipane now appeared on the stairs that lifted the garden a couple of metres above the road. His trousers were acceptable, but his shirt was a disaster and the jacket he carried slung over one shoulder was not much better. His face combined a damp brow with dark shadow on cheeks he had probably shaved that morning.

When he approached, Corso stood up. There was not enough room on the bench for three, though Arcadipane gave no sign of wanting to sit down. Isa stood up too.

"If you two sit here much longer, one of those women will call the police!" He indicated the mothers in the play area and laughed, but was clearly in no mood for merriment.

"I haven't much time," he said, helping himself to a loose cigarette from his pocket. "What is it you want?"

"The Snoring Beauties," Corso said.

Arcadipane lit up and took a pull that to him must have been like a draught of fresh water. The city was coming back to life after the siesta under an African air.

"What the fuck are you talking about?"

"It was a house where—" Isa started.

"What's this I'm hearing?" Arcadipane cupped his hand round his ear. "It seems to be the voice of someone whose mouth should be shut." He leaned towards the girl. "Haven't you already spent enough time fucking everything up? You had to go to the Carabinieri! You can't even imagine the shit you deserve. All we need now is to ask the Carabinieri for favours. And then go on a pilgrimage to Lourdes!"

Corso waited for Arcadipane to calm down. The commissario took three long pulls at his cigarette, then passed a hand over his sweaty brow.

"O.K., what is all this snoring crap?"

Corso told him.

When he had finished, Arcadipane threw his fag end on the ground and watched it smoking.

"I wouldn't even tread in that shit with boots on," he said. He turned to Isa. "You haven't gone and stuck your nose in this already, have you?"

Isa shook her head without looking at him to make it quite clear the subject was of no interest to her. Now the garden was filling with people walking dogs. It was almost six in the evening.

"No investigation necessary," Corso said. "All it needs is for you to spread the word that someone is interested."

Arcadipane looked over at the police car waiting for him. The driver, leaning on the bonnet, was talking into his mobile and laughing. He had dark glasses and the sleeves of his yellow polo shirt were tight on his biceps.

"How can this business have even the faintest connection with Autumnal?" he said. "Be honest."

Corso looked at the swings. The little girl and her nanny had gone. Other little girls and their nannies or mothers were still there, but they did not count.

"As much of a connection as it needs," he said.

34

Corso looked up from his book for the umpteenth time, hoping the butterfly had gone, but it was still where he had last seen it a little earlier, intent on its blind battle against the window.

This is something we should all see, he thought, at least once in a lifetime. Anyone who has a heart, that is, even if their heart is cold and closed like mine.

He had gone down to the school chemistry lab at the beginning of his free period to reread the pages he had circled in pencil during the last few days: an old habit, one of those surviving from his earlier life. He had known the large lab would be in shade and silent at that hour, but no sooner had he opened the book than his attention was distracted by the butterfly. It was not a gaudy one, in fact it was all brown, and its large yellow-edged wings each had a brown eye at the centre. In the minutes during which he watched the distressing tenacity with which the little creature struggled to get through the closed part of the window, ignoring the open half, Corso had had the opportunity to meditate on many things, some of them indefinable, like the fact that "an image may be the more inaccessible the closer we are to it", and that "forty minutes in the life of a butterfly may well correspond to twenty years in the life of a human". Other ideas were firmer but more discouraging: for example, the story of the Snoring Beauties, the only imaginable clue still open, was turning out to be a blind alley, like the D.N.A. of the hair and the signature in the register. In any case, what could he possibly have expected from a story forty years old that was no longer of interest to anyone? In the four days since their meeting in the gardens no more had been heard from Arcadipane, while Isa's research was continuing to end "in shit".

"Let it go," Corso had told her the evening before, when she had called to update him.

"What?"

He was holding the telephone away from his ear because of the hammering beat of the music coming out of it. He imagined her perched on a stool, her breasts pressed against the edge of a bar.

"I said let it go," he repeated.

Isa paused, presumably to take a swig, or perhaps just to stare at the wet mark her glass had made on the bar.

Finally she spoke. "Why don't we go back to Luda, throw the story of the snoring girls in his face?"

Corso drank a mouthful of the instant coffee he had taken with him to the phone. During the last few days he had worked out three reasons for not going back to Luda and arranged them in order of importance. But it was late and he did not feel like discussing the subject at length.

"Arcadipane's right," was all he allowed himself to say. "The snoring girls may not be connected with Autumnal in any way. No point in stirring up a hornets' nest for nothing."

"It's not fucking nothing! Those men were screwing children!"

"Not so far as we know. And anyway they were children forty years ago."

"So?"

"The statute of limitations kicks in after ten years."

"Then why are you forcing me to keep struggling, and why do you keep kicking Arcadipane in the balls?"

Corso took a second mouthful of instant coffee and said nothing, leaving her time to choose what to say next. The milk he had put in his coffee had been open for days. Even by the feeble light of his lamp he could see little white filaments floating on the black.

"What are you doing?" Isa asked eventually.

"In what sense?"

"In the sense of now."

Her slow, velvety voice floated over the banality of the music, like a foulard drifting on the oily waters of a port.

"I'm finishing my coffee."

"And then?"

"I shall read Kawabata."

"And after that?"

"I shall try to sleep."

He had identified the soporific tinkle of ice in the glass Isa was lifting to her lips. It was a thick glass. Whisky, probably. He remembered that noise. A beautiful sound, though remembering it was less beautiful. He heard Isa take two rapid, decisive swigs.

"Good boy," she had said before ringing off. "Read your Kawabullshit, then go to sleep."

Corso got up and went to the window. The butterfly was resting quietly, perhaps in preparation for its next attempt. A combination of beauty and helplessness, unable either to destroy itself or rise to the challenge.

Autumnal is like that too, he thought, approaching the butterfly with his index finger.

The butterfly flew up at once. Corso guided it to the open side of the window. The insect contemplated the world outside, perhaps responding to its breath or perhaps to its voice, and it was as if the butterfly was assuming an expression of regret. The expression old people take on in the presence of excess.

"I had no idea you were here!"

Monica was half in the corridor and half in the room. They studied one another calmly.

"It's not true," she was smiling. "I did know. I wanted to say sorry. It's just that . . ."

"Everything's in place," Corso said.

". . . when I see you like this, it's not my business, but . . ."

"It's O.K. You were right."

"A bit yes, though . . ."

"Monica?"

"Yes."

"Everything's fine."

"Sure?"

"Sure."

She joined her hands as if in prayer, as if to say "really sure?"

"Sure."

"Good! I was afraid you didn't want me as your friend anymore. Why are you holding your finger like that?"

Corso glanced at his index finger, which was still pointing at the world into which the butterfly had returned. He shook his head to indicate it was nothing, put his hand in his pocket and went out of the room.

They went along the corridor and up the stairs and finally reached the second floor, surrounded by the general uproar caused by the bell. Corso had his bag on his shoulder and the book in his hand. He was wearing mountaineering trousers with rectangular patches on the knees, and his usual check shirt. Monica wore a cloth bag round her neck and a maize-coloured blouse, her hair fastened back with a red pencil. Despite the obstruction of her long skirt, her legs were moving with the harmony beautiful legs always have and ugly legs never do. Corso understood that kind of beauty. It was like living near the sea or at the edge of a lake, or walking beside a river. Something that works ceaselessly inside you, even when you are thinking of something entirely different.

They stopped at the foot of the stairs.

"What are you reading?"

Corso showed her the book.

"Japanese?"

"Absolutely."

Monica leafed through it till she came to one of the phrases he had underlined.

"'To the old, death; to the young, love; only one death, but many loves.' Comforting! What's all that about?"

"About old men who spend the night beside sleeping girls."

"Lots of sex?"

"Apparently not."

"Forget it, then," she said, giving the book back to him. Tomorrow we're taking class three to the Gallery of Modern Art, remember?"

"Can't I get out of that?"

"You said you'd be free to come."

"When?"

"At the staff meeting before last."

"Since when have I left it to you to decide such things?"

"I thought you'd like to come into Turin with me. We're friends, aren't we?"

"Something of the sort."

"Something of the sort is good enough for me." She turned and smiled at him. "The station at eight, then."

Corso climbed the final flight of stairs and headed for his class.

From inside came the usual heavy sound of voices, restlessness, and chairs scraping the floor. The atmosphere in the corridor was static and electric, as in all places that fill and empty in a hurry.

Seeing no-one near the door, Corso assumed the students must all be in the school hall for some meeting he had forgotten about. But when he came into the room he found them all sitting in their places. The buzz among the desks died down.

"What's going on?"

Some stared at him in silence, while others looked down at their books, which were already open: most unusual. A couple of boys were laughing with their heads down.

He went to the teacher's desk, took out one of the three pens in his pocket and started calling the register, but looks were resting on him like the light but sharp feet of a bird.

"Well?" he said, looking up from the list of absentees. A girl who in no way resembled her name, which was Elisabetta, settled her hands on her desk.

"Have you really done these things?" she said.

Bramard had no idea what she was talking about, but her obscure words could bode no good, especially in public. The class were rustling discreetly like a flock of sheep shut up in their pen. Some were looking out of the window.

He went over to find out what they were looking at.

The clock on the tower between the buildings in the centre showed just after one. It was a hot day, though not excessively so, the sky veiled with clouds with frayed edges. Soon the large umbrellas in the market that lent colour to the piazza would be beginning to close, and the two lines of cars parked at the sides of the avenue would be thinning out. Down in the courtyard, the children from the primary school were doing everything children do when they know they'll be free in half an hour.

Something written up in red beside the coach stop caught his eye.

He was overcome by a sudden drowsiness, his hands on the window ledge felt tired and he longed with his whole body to sit down, shut out the light, close the door and sleep.

But his eyes were drawn back to those words that had not been there the day before: BRAMARD MURDERER WASN'T TWO ENOUGH?

Corso bowed his head, something he did when he needed to think fast. His first thought was: *We're there!* Then: *But I wouldn't have believed it.* And finally: *I should have taken it into account.*

All the other thoughts that now crowded in rapidly related to things that must now be done and he developed them as he crossed the three metres and twenty-five centimetres between the window and the door.

35

The telephone had been ringing for a long time. It was the second time Bramard had rung. It had been about two minutes since he first tried to get through: the time he had had to wait for the only traffic light on the way out of the village to turn green.

"Hello?" Finally his uncle answered.

"Corso here."

"I was outside hitching up the cart."

"I need you to do two things for me, quickly."

"What's going on?"

"I'll tell you later, but go at once to the bar. Elena should be there working. Don't say anything to her, but make sure no-one's taking an undue interest in her, then stay on till I get there. If she wants to go because she's finished work, don't let her leave, tell her she must wait for me. But if she's not there, go to her house and wait outside it till I come. If you see a car or anyone else there, go into her house and call me. Is that clear?"

"I think so."

"Before you go, take the Luger, load it and carry it with you. But don't use it, no matter what happens. I just want you to have it ready to give to me when I get there."

"If I have to hurry I can only do either one thing or the other."

"Why?"

"Because the Luger's not here, I'd have to go and get it."

Corso thought.

"Then forget the Luger, just go to the bar."

"So I should go to the bar?"

"Yes, at once."

He turned off his mobile phone and looked at the time. He would be there in about twenty minutes, his uncle a little before him. He slowed down as he passed through the only built-up area on the way: a place of a few thousand inhabitants with three restaurants, only one of them any good, a tobacconist's belonging to someone who had been in the same class as him at school, two hairdressers – one with a shop, the other working from home – a mechanic, a car-body repairer, a large workshop where they manufactured chassis for car transporters and employed more than twenty workers, a building society, a grocer, a bar with three fruit machines and a state lottery office. Also the foundations of a petrol pump that had been begun but never finished because of credit problems, a funeral parlour, a church, a kindergarten run by a mother with an ancient teaching diploma and a glass eye and a daughter with an up-to-date certificate of education – and a primary school.

Emerging from the built-up area, Corso looked in his wallet for the ticket with the phone number, but realising he could not simultaneously read it, dial the number and drive, he moved to the side of the road and slowed down.

Isa answered: "Yes."

Corso accelerated again, throwing up gravel.

"They've made a move."

"How?"

"Written up something outside the school where I teach."

He read out the words to her.

"Autumnal?"

"No."

"How can you be sure?"

"Not his style."

"Then who was it? They can't all be either dead or decrepit."

"No matter. When you said there's a file on me, was that true?"

"Why the fuck would I have said there's a file if there wasn't?"

"What's written there?"

"What I told you."

"Nothing else?"

Isa said nothing. In his time Corso had learnt to understand why people stay silent. This was the category of silence that means the person really has nothing more to say. But he needed to be sure.

"In the file, does it say anything about a relationship with a woman?"

"What woman?"

"Does it say anything, or not?"

"No, there's nothing there."

"I've got something I have to sort out now. I'll get back to you this evening."

"And in the meantime what the fuck do I do?"

Corso swung south from the main road. The surrounding countryside was getting greener after several nights of rain and fresh mornings. Inspiring if you had nothing else to worry about.

"You watch Luda," he told Isa. "See whether he has any visitors, and if he goes out check where he goes. Can you do nothing about the telephones?"

"How can I check them when there may still be more calls to come? It'll take a few days."

"O.K., just concentrate on Luda then."

"What about Arcadipane?"

"Has he asked you anything?"

"No."

"Then let's leave him out of it. I'll have a word with him this evening."

"But where are you going?"

Corso could see the village in the distance. He didn't look in the direction of his own house or his uncle's. No extraneous thoughts, no looking back, only the present and a trajectory that would carry him a few metres further on. It had been a long time since he had last functioned in that manner. He hadn't believed he was still capable of it.

"Only call me if something happens," he told Isa. "Otherwise wait for me to get in touch."

36

They had been half an hour on the road, during which time neither had said a word.

Corso had already said most of what he had to say in the kitchen, trying to get Elena to throw some things into a bag and come with him, while Elena kept saying that she was going nowhere without an explanation. In the end they agreed Corso would tell her everything in the car.

But it hadn't gone that way, at least not so far. Once in the car Elena had closed herself up with her own thoughts, her head against the window and her bag in her lap, giving way to an exhaustion she seemed unable to put off any longer.

Corso, for his part, had done little to keep his promise: any explanation would have meant going back to the start and he did not feel like doing that. When Elena closed her eyes, he did no more than lower the window a little and tear his eyes from her sleeping face, and that beauty she shared with deer, predatory animals, wolves, dogs, beetles and elephants. Animals elegantly dangerous. Rapid without ever losing their composure. Terrible yet capable of enduring fidelity too.

"Does Adrian have any part in this story?" she asked suddenly.

"Who's Adrian?"

Elena kept her eyes closed and did not answer.

"No," Corso said, understanding. "He's not involved."

They were travelling fast towards a horizon lined with mountains. There was no traffic. Occasional agricultural buildings and fortifications perched up high like stacked boxes interrupted cultivated stretches of kiwi fruits and apple trees.

"How long will this take?" Elena asked.

"An hour."

"I don't mean the journey. How long do I have to stay?"

"It's just a precaution. I hope to sort everything quickly."

"And he's the danger?"

"He who?"

"I know what happened to you. Did you think no-one in the village has ever talked about it?"

Corso slowed down. In front of him was the stern of a yacht, its rudder lashed in place with white cord. The boat was partly concealed under a grey cloth on a trailer. Pulling the trailer was a jeep with very large wheels. He moved to the left to overtake, but there a tractor was coming in the opposite direction, so he reduced his speed and dropped back.

"No. This is a different story."

Elena lifted her head from the window and zipped up her bag. It wasn't nearly full, she had only picked up a few things from the bathroom and her bedroom.

"What story? What has it got to do with me?"

"Nothing, but someone might want to get at anyone close to me."

Corso felt her eyes running from his temple down his arms, finally stopping at his hands on the steering wheel. He had known her eyes rest like that on him before, but only in the dark.

"I'm really sorry," he said. "I never wanted this."

He checked what was coming in the opposite direction and changed lane. The man driving the Land Rover was about forty and bald, and wore the collar of his polo up, a style Corso had always found irritating. Returning to his own lane he looked into his rear-view mirror where something else had attracted his attention. He looked again after another hundred metres. And after a kilometre.

"I'm going to stop for some petrol," he said, seeing a service station. "Do you need the bathroom?"

"No."

"Then stay in the car."

Corso drove up to a pump where a notice clearly announcing SERVICE was in full view, got out and went to unscrew the cap of his petrol tank. No other cars had stopped to fill up. The sky was overcast and an unsteady wind had caught a notice about collecting coupons.

The little man who worked the pump hurried over.

"O.K., you can leave that to me!" the man said.

Corso moved aside to make room for him.

With his little moustache and bulging eyes, the man looked like an American film actor, though an actor would never have allowed himself the hairy mole he had on his cheek. He smiled. It was clear that he had had some other occupation he had no intention of returning to, and that for him being promoted to petrol pump attendant was a sign that he was a beneficiary of the new good times.

"How much shall we put in?"

"Fill her up," Corso said. "Anywhere I can wash my hands?"

Almost dancing, the attendant inserted the nozzle into the Polar. A packet of Marlboros stuck out of the pocket of his sponsored overalls.

"Of course," he said. "Round the back. The door doesn't lock, but it says 'Occupied'."

On his way to the toilet Corso took a look at the road, the hardware store on the other side, an eating place advertising

173

TWO COURSES, WATER & COFFEE € 8.50 with a space in front of it where a decorator's van, five cars and two small lorries were parked.

Then he turned the corner to the back of the service station.

There were some gas cylinders, three tyres, the manager's car, and an iron chest full of iron objects. He peered into this. Mostly it contained brake discs, but there were also screws, broken windscreen-wipers and an aluminium pipe, probably from some sort of gas installation. He picked this up and bent it one way and another against the edge of the chest until he managed to break off a short piece, which he put in his pocket. He threw the rest back where he had found it, went into the toilet, washed his hands and returned to the car.

The little man waiting by the pump was looking worried. His overalls exaggerated his shoulders to a ridiculous degree.

"It would only take seven litres fifty," he said, irritated. "Your tank was almost full."

Corso paid.

Once he had the money in his hand, the man seemed to take heart. He opened a worn leather wallet, and slipped the ten-euro note in among others of higher denominations.

"Shall I check the oil?" he asked, glancing at the woman sitting in the car, who had been staring at the mountains all the while.

"No need," Corso said.

"O.K.," the attendant nodded. "It's best to do some things for oneself."

Corso stared at him without moving. The man stopped grinning and smoothed down his oily hair.

"Come and see us again," he said before retreating to his kiosk, walking like a man who expects a brick in his back at any moment.

Corso knocked on the window and Elena lowered it.

"Now you drive," he said.

"I haven't got my licence with me."

"Doesn't matter."

Elena threw her bag onto the back seat and got behind the steering wheel. Before getting in beside her, Corso slightly adjusted his wing mirror.

After about ten kilometres they reached the valley Corso was aiming for. Elena was driving slowly, her eyes on the road. Corso looked in the mirror from time to time. The fruit trees had given way to ash trees. A harmless ivory light was filtering through the clouds.

"Take the next right," Corso said.

"Where?"

"This little road here."

Elena turned onto a small asphalted road. Dividing a field in two, the little road twisted sharply at first, but soon relaxed into a series of regular corners. Its surface, eroded by rain and ice, creaked beneath the tyres.

"Now listen carefully," Corso said. "When I tell you, you must stop. I'll get out of the car and you must drive on immediately."

He paused to be sure Elena had understood. She looked at him, then back at the road.

"Go another fifty metres then stop, but stay in the car in the middle of the road and keep the engine running. Don't turn round. Do nothing else, just wait."

"How far is fifty metres?"

"As far as that hut near the water."

"Can't I wait where you get out?"

"No, do as I say, I'll be back almost at once."

"Shall I stop now?"

Corso looked at the vegetation on his right. The bank at that point was too steep and the trees were sparse enough for the bottom of the valley where the main road passed to be visible. Not even the bushes and brambles growing under the trees offered any cover.

"Not yet," he said.

After a turn to the left, the road stretched out ahead. Corso let Elena drive on about another twenty metres.

"Stop here," he said.

She did so.

"Then fifty metres more," Corso repeated, his door already open.

He quickly reached a clump of buddleia at the side of the road, and from there watched the Polar draw away.

That's less than forty metres, he thought, when he saw it stop. No matter.

He turned to look back at the curve they had just come by. Despite the noise of the Polar's engine, he could hear the other car approaching. Petrol. Medium power. There was no sound from the wood. He could hear the car climbing, then it appeared, green and cautious, from the curve. A Lancia of sportive appearance, but not of the highest class. Five doors, as he had hoped.

When the man at the wheel became aware of the Polar motionless in the middle of the road he stopped without breaking sharply, then leaned calmly towards the windscreen to judge the distance. He was about sixty, with a thin, deliberate face, a man not likely to be easily surprised by life.

Realising it was too late for him to retreat he relaxed into his seat, took some cigarettes from the dashboard and deftly flicked one from the packet to his lips with the gesture of a film actor.

He was just lighting it when the door behind him opened, and before he had time to turn he felt something cold pressed against his neck under his right ear. He held the lighter suspended in mid-air long enough to show he had got the message, then finished lighting his cigarette and put the lighter back in the dashboard.

"Not a gun, I think," he said into his first puff of smoke.

"Maybe," said Corso. "Turn off the engine."

"In any case, no gun is needed. We're both of the old school, aren't we?"

"I said turn off the engine."

The man, who had grey hair, cheeks scarred from youth by acne and an attractive voice, did as he was told.

"Why are you following us?"

"My job," he said, blowing smoke from his mouth in the manner of one for whom a cigarette is a combination of rival, confessor and sister.

"What kind of job?"

"May I?" the man said, raising his hands.

"Do you have a gun?"

"Not my style. I told you that."

Corso glanced ahead to the Polar. It seemed Elena had not turned to look. The stop lights were on, so her foot must be on the brake.

"O.K."

The man pulled a brown leather wallet from the inside pocket of his jacket and handed it to Corso, who opened it and read the name beside the photograph and the official stamp of the prefecture of Rimini: Callisto Reggio, private detective. Corso looked at the date of birth, closed the wallet and put it on his knee.

"Who are you working for?"

"You know I can't tell you that."

"You'll have to tell the police."

"The police, maybe. In any case, intermediaries contact me, so I don't know exactly who I'm working for."

"Their telephone number?"

"I don't have a number for them. And I'm paid by courier."

"A man or a woman?"

"A man."

"Age?"

"Not young, I'd say."

"Accent? Special features of pronunciation?"

"None."

Corso looked down at the man's shoes. Good quality, a bit retro. Decent taste. Tawny and well-worn. He had said, "In any case," twice: a conciliatory, diplomatic type, not contentious.

"What did he ask you to do?"

"Follow you and report back, nothing more."

"Is that all?"

"That's all."

"And the words written on the wall?"

The man shook his head.

"Nothing to do with me. In this business, I side with the angels."

A leaf fluttered down on the bonnet. Corso followed its trajectory as far as the green surface, then looked at the Polar, so near and yet so incalculably far away, vulnerable and alone. He thought of the first time he and Elena had been together in the dark when they had done what to him was the nearest thing he had experienced for a very long time to making love.

"Well, what are we going to do?" the man said.

Corso studied his neck. A two-day beard.

"What do you suggest?"

The man threw the remains of his cigarette out of the window.

"I'd suggest we don't meet again," he said.

"Good idea, also because another time I'd have to hurt you."

"With a piece of piping?"

Corso pressed the aluminium tube so that it scratched the man's skin under his ear.

"Now give me your car keys and phone."

"That's not necessary."

"If you really are one of the old school, you know that it is."

The man used his right hand to detach the keys, and gave them to Corso, together with the mobile phone he kept in the radio compartment. The collar of his shirt was stained with two drops of blood. Nothing to speak of.

"Now take off your jacket and lean forward," Corso said.

The man did as he was told. Corso checked that he had no holster round his neck or weapons at his waist. In twenty years as a policeman he had never set eyes on an ankle holster – American crap.

"Open the glove compartment."

Papers and a satnav. No guns.

Corso got out of the car. Up to this point the man really had shown himself to be one of the old school and there was no reason to think he was faking it.

"I don't want to see you again, is that clear?" he said, going up to the window. "Now put the car in neutral."

The man stared at him with his elongated colonial eyes, their whites slightly yellow, perhaps from tobacco smoke. He put the car in neutral and when it began to roll back guided it to the side of the road.

Corso forced himself to walk nonchalantly to the Polar. There were some things he was no longer used to. Being tough was not at all like acting tough.

As soon as she saw him coming, Elena got out of the Polar.

She looked from Corso to the Lancia behind him, then at Corso again.

"All fine," he said. "I'll drive."

Elena walked round the bonnet so as not to get in his way.

Corso got in, threw the man's keys, mobile phone and identity card on the back seat, released the hand brake, and drove as far as the next curve, where he turned.

When they passed the Lancia, Callisto Reggio was sitting in the driving seat with the door open and one foot on the ground, as if waiting for his wife to come back from attending to inconvenient if understandable physical urgencies in the bushes.

37

"Bloody hell, Pedrelli, I've only just . . ."

"It's not Pedrelli."

"Bramard! Are you even phoning me at night now?"

"It's not night."

"One o'clock is night-time. Why are you ringing me at home?"

"Your mobile was off."

"Because I was asleep. How do you come to have this number?"

"It doesn't seem to have changed in twenty years."

"Of course not. Do I have to move house now to stop you phoning me?"

"You don't have to move house to change your number."

"Why should I change my number? You throw it away. Why the fuck are you calling me at this hour? Even if Isa's grabbed you by the balls, you could have waited till tomorrow to moan about it. People have to queue, you know."

"They've revealed themselves."

"Who?"

"There was some graffiti in front of the school this morning."

"What sort of thing?"

"A threat. There's someone who doesn't like me sticking my nose into the business of the Snoring Beauties."

"Who the hell?"

"No idea. But someone who knows my past and who my friends are."

"How? Who are your friends?"

"Never mind. I've sorted that."

"Then why the hell are you phoning me? Mariangela has to be up at six."

"Because you must have told someone I was interested in the Snoring Beauties."

"No. I looked into the archives and spoke to a couple of retired colleagues. There was nothing in the archives, but things were said at the time. A little fun for politicians and business-men, a pregnant underage girl, sorted out by marrying her off to a boy happy to accept the child with a dowry, parents paid off too, everyone happy. End of story. Can I go to sleep now?"

"I need you to check out a private detective for me."

"I can't stand private detectives, you know that."

"Callisto Reggio, born September 15, 1952. Probably a bit behind me. Licensed by Rimini prefecture. Find out what he usually does and at what level, and whether he has any connec-tion with the police or public services. I can give you his telephone number. Check any calls made during the last fifteen days."

"Sure you don't want a blow job while we're about it? I'm now wide awake and haven't cleaned my teeth yet."

"And send Isa to photograph what is written on the wall at the school. We can compare the writing, though I'm sure this isn't the man we're after."

"Isn't Isa on speaking terms with you anymore?"

"How soon can you have something for me?"

"No idea."

"Good."

"What d'you mean, good? What are you up to now?"

"Just waiting. Sooner or later they'll make another move."

"You mean they'll kill you?"

"I don't think so. I'll call you tomorrow."

"Don't call me, I'll call you."

"If you like."

"Corso?"

"Yes."

"I've got three open murders on my plate. Try not to get yourself killed just to fuck me up even when you're dead."

Arcadipane put down the phone and shuffled back down the corridor in his underpants, vest, socks and the boiled-wool slippers his children had given him for Christmas and he hadn't put away despite the change of season. The first time he had seen them he'd been disappointed that his children had chosen slippers, particularly with wedge heels, but Christmas is not the time to question presents. Then as the weeks passed he had grown fond of them. They were comfortable and warm. And also the only thing he had that was grey, and the only thing with a flower in relief on it.

In the bedroom he did not turn on the light, but slipped off his slippers and got back into bed.

"Is he in trouble?" said his wife.

"Oh no." Arcadipane drew the sheet up to his chin, "not at all."

"What's going on, then?"

"Nothing. Go to sleep."

Mariangela moved closer to her husband. The fact that they had been married for twenty years and that she slept with her back to him and did not share his ideas about what to do on Sundays, had never detracted from other aspects of their life together.

"Anyone would find it difficult to adjust after what happened to him."

Arcadipane put his left hand under his neck and closed his eyes.

"We've already discussed this endlessly."

"You shouldn't be so hard on him."

He opened his eyes again.

"I'm not hard on him. I'm the only person who listens to him."

He closed his eyes again.

"Don't you ever give it any serious thought?"

"How do you mean?"

"What if it had happened to you?"

"No. Particularly not just before I go to sleep."

Silence.

"But you must think about it sometimes."

"Of course I do." He reopened his eyes abruptly. "But I try not to. Now go to sleep, it's late and you have to get up early."

He put one foot round the calf of her leg. His feet were strong and sensitive, like the limbs of some marine animal that probably never had limbs.

"It's not that late," Mariangela said.

Arcadipane turned on his side and put an arm round her. The weight of her drooping breasts against his hand excited him.

"The kids have a free afternoon tomorrow," she whispered. "When will you be home?"

"At two."

"I'll get away and come home to meet you."

"But I'm randy now. Aren't you?"

"Of course I am."

"You're only saying that to please me."

"To please you? Can't you tell?"

She was quiet for a while.

"How can it be possible I still turn you on?"

"What kind of a question is that?"

"I've never been a beauty, but at least I used to have a good bum and boobs. My legs are so fat now." She smoothed down the duvet to outline her figure.

"You still have a nice big bum."

"A nice big bum isn't a beautiful big bum."

"You still have a beautiful big bum and everything else big and beautiful as well."

"But my boobs?"

"They always turn me on. Now go to sleep."

"O.K., but it's a shame."

"I know, but I'm sure I'll feel the same tomorrow. Just have to remember not to eat too much for lunch."

"So now we go to sleep?"

"Yes."

"Can you?"

"I can if you can."

"Goodnight, then."

"Yes, goodnight now."

For a little longer Arcadipane contemplated what he could see of his wife in the weak light coming through the shutters, conscious of the smell of her skin and the rebellious curl of hair under her ear. He had always loved her skin, her hair, her ability to fall asleep so quickly and the fact that she was always as good as her word.

Just look at her! he told himself.

Any woman could fall asleep beside a barman, a teacher or even a thief, but sleeping regularly with a policeman was something else. It was something policemen, assassins and a few other occupations shared, that it was not easy for women to sleep beside them.

Bramard had known that sleeping was never going to be easy

for him again after what happened to him. And Arcadipane too would have been unable to sleep at all without Mariangela.

Look at her, he said to himself. She sleeps like a child.

She had put on weight and her hair was going grey, but it would not have put him off her if she had lost a leg, turned blind or had to take pills as big as your hand. When you have his sort of work, you really need a woman capable of being the first to fall asleep.

And if you have the good fortune to find one and then lose her, you can beat your head against a brick wall, but you'll never again be able to sleep the way you could when you had her.

There, he thought, finally allowing his worried features to relax. That's enough thinking about what I can't help thinking about.

He caressed his wife one last time, took a deep breath and fell asleep, serene in the knowledge that he had pushed the wheelbarrow to the top of the hill and now all he had to do was go down the other side.

38

"What does the title of the picture mean?"

Corso looked from the painting to the profile of the girl who had come to stand at his side.

"Daphne was the woman's name," he said.

"Her real name?"

"Daphne Maugham. She was English. Pavarolo is where she lived with the painter. They were married. She was a painter too."

The girl nodded, still looking at the woman sitting on the window ledge in the painting.

Corso had known this girl for a couple of years. She was good at foreign languages, but struggled with History. Her father had a fruit stall in the market.

"Do you watch 'A Couch for Two'?" the girl said.

"Is that a T.V. programme?"

"Yes."

"No, I don't know it."

"Every afternoon a celebrity sits on the couch with the presenter, who's called Gabriella, and she asks them questions about their life, and at the end she gives them a portrait of themselves done by an artist in half an hour. I don't understand how they can do such a good picture so quickly."

One of the girl's friends called her, but she went on staring at the painting.

"Sometimes I pretend to answer the presenter's questions: where I was born, what my parents were like, when I discovered my talent and whether success changed my life. I always say I went on being a normal person, doing the shopping, seeing my friends, living with my family, same as everyone else."

The girl's friend called her again. She turned and said she would come in a minute.

"It's very good that you keep your feet on the ground.

The girl nodded. "I have to go now. Are you going to stay here?"

"Yes, a bit longer."

The girl rejoined the group around the guide and the teacher of Business Administration at the other end of the hall. On reaching the first abstract paintings most of the students had begun to drop back, grumbling about sore feet. Corso knew he ought to round them up, but he could not take his eyes off the woman in the painting. The image related in some way to something struggling to surface in his mind involving desire and at the same time regret.

"Shall we collect the stragglers?"

"Yes," Corso said, but as he turned towards Monica his eyes fell on the hands of the woman clasped over her knee in the painting and he remembered.

One night many years ago he had woken in a bed not his own, and after lying for a long time in silence, had begun moving through the rooms in that unfamiliar house.

In the semi-darkness he had studied photographs that showed the woman, the man and the small boy whose home it was, the small aide-memoire notices pinned to a cork board, and the little objects these people used in their everyday domestic life. He sat a long time on the edge of the bath staring at the razor, the shaving cream, the toothbrushes and the child's

Spider-Man toothpaste. The night was nearly over and the shadow of a magnolia projected by a street-lamp was moving to and fro beyond the frosted glass of the window.

Then Corso imagined the father and the small boy that these objects belonged to waking in the guesthouse where they had gone for the weekend, and though the boy was only eleven, eating their breakfast in silence like two grown men. Then they would go down to the beach early enough to reach the water before other bathers scared away the fish, and at midday would sit on the rocks eating focaccia, their clothes spread out to dry beside them in the sun.

It was the one and only time in his life that Corso had cried.

Cried for Michelle and Martina, lost five years before, but also because beauty more than anything else needs to be intact, and once it is lost there can never be any remedy or meaningful consolation.

Coming back into the bedroom, he had seen the woman sitting on the windowsill, the hills beginning to appear behind her in the early dawn. Hearing him come in, she had turned her head, and they stared at each other, he naked and in tears at the door, she also with wet eyes and her hands clasped over her knee, her breasts outlined through her dressing gown by the light from beyond. Then he had dressed, and saying nothing, left the house for ever, home to the only person who had ever seen him cry.

"Well? What is it?" Monica said.

"Nothing," Corso said. "Let's go."

They traced the same route in reverse, discovering students collapsed on benches like survivors of an inglorious retreat stopping to get their breath back somewhere where all they can be aware of is how very far from home they are. Monica persuaded them to follow her by promising the visit was nearly over, dragging them to the last room, where most of them had gathered in front of a painting by Emilio Vedova that had only two patches of colour.

This reunited the reluctant with the recalcitrant, though not without a few acrimonious glances between the two groups. The guide was about to resume her explanatory patter, but hardly had time to begin speaking before her voice was drowned by the shrill scream of an alarm.

Everyone looked round ready to laugh or complain, but the room was otherwise empty, white and clean, and nothing in it had moved.

Corso looked for the shaved head of Alviano, finding it as always close to the curly hair of Cammarata.

The two had been moving in unison like a pre-war comedy act: Cammarata tall, thin, sickly and always on the verge of astonishment; Alviano big-boned, lumpy, with the face of a deserter, a half-smoked cigarette permanently between his lips. In age they were separated by three years because Alviano had been failed twice and had also taken a year out to work as a builder, but some strange alchemy united them. Now both were laughing and looking at their feet.

Corso took two steps towards them.

A blue-uniformed attendant had come into the room. With everyone watching, he went to a concealed door in the white wall, opened it and stopped the alarm. Then before leaving he reminded them in a bored voice not to go near the canvases because they were protected by an alarm system.

The guide then began once more to talk about the historical period that had fostered that type of picture. Some of the students were listening while others were staring at the back, the bottom or the head of hair of whoever was in front of them. A Japanese visitor had come into the room.

Corso noticed that Alviano and Cammarata had shifted

slightly. He moved to the right to get a better view of them, but when Alviano reached a hand towards the painting he had no time to do or say anything.

This time when the alarm went off the guide looked irritated, but realising there was nothing she could do, simply dropped her eyes disconsolately, like a Madonna contemplating the plundering of her own church from the altar.

Corso looked at Alviano, who was laughing with his head shrunk into his shoulders.

He took a step towards him, but before he could get there the teacher of Business Administration came face-to-face with the boy.

The two stared at each other for a moment, then the woman said something sharp but indistinct, only the final word ringing out clearly through the room at the exact moment when the attendant stopped the alarm.

". . . cretin!"

The students all turned and nothing more was heard except the cautiously retreating steps of the attendant in the blue uniform. Even the Japanese visitor stopped.

Corso reached Alviano.

"Let's go," he said.

The boy was holding the cold stare of the female teacher.

She was quite a lot shorter than he was, a thin woman who had two young daughters and liked to come to school on her bicycle – though at the present moment she seemed transformed into pure aggression.

"Let's go," Corso said again.

Alviano took a step back, like a large herbivore anxious to escape from a dangerous position but afraid to turn its back on a predator. Then, when instinct allowed, he turned and left the room.

Corso followed him back through several rooms, down the stairs and across the gangway over the ticket desk. The gallery's terrace overlooked a small garden where in good weather visitors could sit and leaf through books bought in the bookshop or walk among flowerbeds. Though on this particular grey morning everything was covered by a thin patina of solitude.

Corso looked up at the building facing them. On one balcony, a solicitous hand had wrapped an olive tree in a protective veil of organdie and forgotten to remove it when the winter ended. The grey sky was producing a rain so fine it could only be seen against a dark background.

"That woman can't call me a cretin!" Alviano said from the bench where he had immediately sat down. The Winston he had been forced to abandon half-smoked when they went into the gallery was already back between his lips.

"Maybe not the best idea," Corso said, "but at a certain age you are a cretin if you do certain things, and you have very nearly reached that age."

Alviano looked down, blowing out smoke that dispersed when it touched the ground. A trolleybus passed down the avenue. A car horn sounded, stopped, then sounded again.

"I don't know why I do things like that," he said.

Corso leaned both hands on the window ledge and looked at the garden. On the other side of the glass window, students were reclaiming their bags and backpacks from the cloakroom. Soon they would be emerging in little groups to light cigarettes and turn on their mobiles under the shelter and cast glances in their direction.

"Perhaps you ought to . . ." Corso started, then stopped abruptly. On the grey grass of the garden, at the foot of a tree, was a circle of crimson flowers, all still intact.

"*Chiri tsubaki*," he murmured.

"Eh?" Alviano looked up.

Corso admired the perfect symmetry of the flowers. The bush itself seemed to be leaning towards them in satisfaction, as though having generated the flowers in winter and losing them when they were still intact had made it possible for them to be preserved for ever from death and decay.

"Where are you going, professor?" Alviano called, seeing Corso suddenly cross the terrace with rapid steps. "What shall I say to that Business Studies woman? . . . Professor? Where are you going?"

39

"I was waiting for your call. I'd have got in touch with you earlier, madam, if I'd been able to."

"But you weren't able to, you tell me."

"I'm in an awkward position. This is the first time this has happened to me."

"Is he aware of this?"

"Yes."

"To what extent?"

"Completely, I'd say."

"In what sense?"

"Well, we had a chat."

"A chat?"

"I don't know what to say, I was following them by car . . ."

"I don't mean to be unsympathetic, but I have no interest whatever in your professional details, just tell me about the chat."

"He wanted to know who I was working for and in what capacity. To the first question I had nothing to say, to the second I adjusted myself in some sense to the circumstances. He took my identification card and mobile phone, I suppose he'll have his friend the commissario check them. Your idea of getting in touch with me in this place and on set days and at set times seemed to me an excessive precaution, but now I must admit that—"

"You said *you* were following *them*?"

"He was with his girlfriend, I think taking her somewhere for safety. Yesterday something not very encouraging had been written up near the school. Probably the story of the sleeping girls has annoyed someone."

"Presumably you remember what was written up?"

"*Bramard murderer wasn't two enough.* As far as Bramard is concerned I've obviously burned my boats, but I could still conduct a few relevant enquiries, if you like."

"No, don't bother. Anything else from your chat?"

"So that he would believe things I don't know, I had to tell him a bit of the truth."

"Such as?"

"He knows you're a man."

"Anything else?"

"He doesn't seem too upset by what's happened. Almost as if he expected it."

"That matters even less. Nothing else?"

"No."

"The final payment will reach you by the usual courier. For the next couple of weeks still go to the same place on Mondays and Thursdays. I shan't call you anymore, but it will serve to justify your regular presence there in recent times."

"Forget the payment. I can't enjoy it if I'm not satisfied with my work."

"During these months you have done your job and you will receive what was agreed. If the police should want to see you . . ."

"Only a remote chance, I'd say."

"But if they did . . ."

"I'd have nothing to tell them. To me you are just a voice."

"Good."

They rang off simultaneously, crowning an affinity they had

been aware of from their first phone conversation. An affinity from which both, in the course of a few days or perhaps even a few hours, would erase the fact that they had ever spoken to each other at all.

40

The room he had been sitting in for about twenty minutes was the same as before – the smell of plastic, soundproof walls and neon lighting – but this time, when the door opened to admit Isa and Arcadipane, Corso had on the table before him a yellowed card, Kawabata's novel, a small notepad and a pencil.

Outside the rain was tired and impenitent, oblivious to the fact that it was early June and the last two weeks of school. Corso, leaving home that morning, had acted with the same insouciance, taking no jacket, hat or umbrella. His shirt, sandals and light trousers were swiftly soaked, though he had a plastic bag around his backpack to protect something that must not be allowed to get wet.

Isa sat on his right, the commissario on his left, and the empty side of the table faced the door, on which there was a NO SMOKING sign.

"Umbrellas too middle-class for you?" Arcadipane said.

Pushing wet hair from his forehead and then, as if completing the same gesture by taking up his pencil, Corso wrote a word on the first page of his notepad, which he slid towards the girl.

"Please find a picture of it."

Arcadipane took an ashtray and a cigarette packet from his pocket.

"Three left," he said, peering into the packet. "That gives you ten minutes."

He was the only one with dry clothes and shoes, a sign that he had been working since dawn, if not all night. The ashtray bore the police logo. Service heraldry. Corso relaxed when the first ash fell onto it.

"There," Isa said.

He leaned over to look at her computer screen.

"Enlarge it," he said, without giving the matter much thought.

The girl did so. That morning she was wearing simple trousers and a man's brown shirt, the collar a dark rim where rain had got in between her helmet and her jacket. No marks, slashes or pins with threatening slogans. And her usual waterproofs.

When Isa had finished, Corso turned the screen towards the commissario.

"These are the flowers of *Camellia Japonica*, a plant originally from Japan that flowers in autumn and winter. The remarkable thing about its flowers is that they fall to the ground intact in spring."

Arcadipane took a quick glance at the red flowers.

"But!" He held up his cigarette as if to remind a competitor of time passing in an hourglass.

Corso smiled weakly. He opened the card on which someone, in handwriting not his own, had written AUTUMNAL, spread six black and white photographic prints out on the table, and bent back the computer screen to face the ceiling.

"Stand up," he said.

"Why?"

"Both of you please stand up."

Arcadipane and Isa stood up.

"What can you see?"

Arcadipane leaned forward, gripping the edge of the table with both hands.

"Some flowers thrown on the ground," he said, "and six pictures I've already seen – more often than I'd like."

Corso waited.

"There's a design," Isa said.

"What design?" Arcadipane squared up to her.

Isa enlarged the computer image twice more.

"The design of the flowers. It's the same as the design on the backs of the women."

Arcadipane pushed his face nearer the screen, then looked more closely at one of the photographs.

"Could be," he admitted. "But what does that mean?"

"It means that Autumnal never slashed at random, but reproduced the pattern of the *chiri tsubaki* on the women's backs."

"The pattern of what?"

"The Japanese name for this type of camellia. In Japan its flowers are considered a symbol of perfection, but also of 'life cut short' in youth."

"So now we know this man understands about flowers. Anything else?"

"The bonsai shrubs the Pontremoli woman has been given in recent years come from the same plant."

The commissario's expression betrayed no surprise. He lifted his cigarette to his lips very slowly, his eyes screwed up as always when his coarse-grained mind was confronted with anything at all subtle.

He put his cigarette down on the ashtray. "This merely confirms that Pontremoli's visitor and Autumnal must be the same person. But we knew that already, didn't we?"

Corso nodded; he knew the commissario needed to reduce everything to the basics to get his mind into gear. He cleared a space on the table and took more black and white photographs from the folder.

"These were taken by the Carabinieri at the Pontremoli home the day the mother threw herself from the balcony. Here's the terrace," he said, putting down the first photograph, "the path," placing the second on top of it, "and the garden."

"And the same plant," Isa said.

"Yes, and I noticed another exactly like it in Luda's garden, when we went to call on him."

"They were obsessed with the Far East," Arcadipane snorted. "They could easily have seen such plants during their travels."

"In fact, there is a very famous *Camellia Japonica* in a temple in Kyoto," Corso said, "but I don't think that's the reason they both had a *chiri tsubaki* in their gardens."

He picked up the book still lying face up on the table, opened it at a place he had marked with an old postcard and read: "*For this reason, in the house of the 'Sleeping Beauties', with the girl's arm over his eyes, Eguchi had seen a vision of* chiri tsubaki *in full flower.*" Then he shut the book and put it back on the table.

Arcadipane stared at him, unable to decide between hostility and resignation, then dragged himself to his feet and began walking about the room. Even though his steps were slow, his short legs denied him any dignity, while his large head waved about on his neck like a mallet.

"Alright, let's admit it," he said. "Those three men were crazy enough to set up a brothel after they read about it in a book. And maybe Tabasso too had the same plant in his garden that Autumnal carved on women and has been giving as presents to the Pentremoli woman . . ." He stopped to lift his cigarette from the ashtray and took a pull on it. For a few moments, the smoke from his lips replaced the clear air above the table.

"But Pontremoli's father and the elder Tabasso have been dead fifteen years, so they can't have sent the most recent letters or taken the plants to the Cottolengo; while Luda, who could have done it, in no way corresponds to the identikit of Autumnal provided by the nuns. Conclusion . . ." – Arcadipane stared at Corso through the gradually thinning smoke – ". . . none of those three could possibly be Autumnal."

The only thing moving was the narrow thread of smoke rising from the cigarette. Then Isa kicked her chair aside and went to lean on the wall, her eyes fixed on the photographs covering the table.

"What a load of shit," she murmured, stripping her right thumb free of sticky tape and sticking it into her mouth.

This reminded Corso of something he had first noticed long ago: that when the mind is driven to its limit in its attempt to understand something, the body nearly always drifts free. One person may talk, one tremble, some gesticulate, others again simply abandon their bodies to the power of whatever happens to be near them at the time – rain, another person, a concerto by Brahms, an approaching tram – but always in a kind of paralysis during which anything can happen to them though it is never anything of deep significance.

In his own case, whenever he had to struggle to understand something that was happening to him, he would hiss on a wavelength that only Michelle, their cat and sometimes Arcadipane could hear.

The evening before, when he had decided to tell them after all this time, had been both terrible and moving.

"None of them is Autumnal," he said.

"No?" hazarded the commissario.

"No, but they trained Autumnal in their own taste and lack of scruples. And once he had become what we know him to be, they left him alone to get on with it by himself, but they were pleased with him and protected him.

Arcadipane looked from Corso to the photographs on the

table, the camellias and finally the cigarette, which was at that moment at its last gasp.

"The Pontremoli son is dead, their daughter's a vegetable, and the Tabasso son not only does not fit the description, but he was only a small boy at the time. None of them can have been visiting the Cottolengo or could have put that hair in the envelope."

Corso eyed the wet marks made by his sandalled feet on the floor.

"The fact is, that hair didn't come from the Pontremoli woman," he said.

"What the fuck do you mean? The D.N.A—"

"—merely proves the hair must have come from someone with the same maternal ancestry."

The commissario's bituminous black eyes held Corso's grey ones for several long, slow, muddy moments.

"But how the fuck . . . ?"

Corso nodded his agreement: it was the stupidest mistake they could have made, but also the most logical and therefore likely to be the most persistent.

Arcadipane took the penultimate cigarette from the packet, stuck it in his mouth and lit it.

"Will we still be able to find him, do you think?"

Corso studied Isa and the thumb she was sucking like a baby between her fighter's lips.

He nodded. "He is certain that we will."

41

"Sorry it's so early, Amedeo, I woke from a dream and felt I had to call you."

"That's fine, dear boy, no problem. Was it a bad dream?"

"Nothing serious. I was watching you leave on a trip."

"A long trip?"

"Yes, to somewhere where no worries could reach you."

"Good, though I really thought I'd have a bit more time."

"So did I, but as you taught me yourself, 'Even short men make long shadows when the day is nearly over.'"

"That's still very true!"

"So sorry to bother you like this."

"No need to be sorry: *fukusui bon ni kaerazu*, isn't that so?"

"Yes, indeed. You can't put spilt water back in the vase."

"And then I've always been a nomad."

"I know, and may you always remain one."

"I always will, dear boy, you can be sure of that."

42

They rang at the gate and settled down to wait.

The last drops were dripping from the trees to the asphalt, shaken down by a gentle wind. It had only been raining a couple of hours, but the sky was still an intense grey, shaped by fat clouds that finally did credit to the variable spring-like nature of the season. A bell had just chimed to mark noon.

"Yes?" The familiar voice.

"Police," Isa said.

The woman hesitated, her training perhaps.

"The signore is not at home."

"Where has he gone?"

"I don't know."

"Fuck 'don't know'. Haven't you got the point? It's the police!"

No answer. Corso, who had been leaning on the Polar, now came forward. Isa moved out of his way.

"Nothing to worry about, signora, we would just like to ask you a few questions. Could you kindly open up for us?"

"I'm sorry. The signore is not at home. I can't open . . ."

Corso looked at his feet. The leather of his sandals had faded, and stained his skin.

"Could you come to the gate, at least?"

The woman thought about it. Corso decided not to give her too long to think it over.

"We shall wait for you," he said.

They moved back from the intercom and retreated to the car, each to the side where he had left his or her door open. Isa rested her weight on her elbows as though on a window ledge and studied the garden beyond the barred gate.

"What if he really isn't here?"

"We'll see."

"What shall we see?"

"Why he isn't here."

"A fine philosophy!"

The woman appeared at the top of the path. A typical domestic servant of Philippine or Indonesian origin, perhaps forty-five years old, short and with long black hair gathered in a tail reaching down to her buttocks. No uniform, just black trousers and a white shirt with short sleeves. When she approached the gate, Corso noticed a mobile phone in her hand.

"Good morning, Ester."

The woman stopped a couple of paces away. She did not seem particularly impressed to hear her own name. Probably she dismissed it as one of the many cunning tricks used in recent years by door-to-door salesmen.

"Signor Luda's not at home, then?"

She nodded. Her trainers were the sort that flashes a light every time the sole touches the ground.

"I suppose he didn't leave any information about where he had gone or when he would be back?"

"He left no information."

She must have taken a lot of trouble to master that polite detachment. In fact, her features were gentle and her hands extraordinarily beautiful. Her Italian, apart from a slight accent, was perfect.

"Did he go out this morning?"

"Yes."

"Very early?"

"Very early."

"Did he take any cases with him?"

"One."

"A large one, I expect."

She nodded. Corso's gaze wandered as if he were not particularly interested in her answers.

"I suppose he took a taxi."

Corso gave the weak smile had served him for years as a tool of the trade.

"Thank you, Ester, you've been very kind."

He got into the car and waited for Isa to register that the interview was over.

When she got in, he started the engine and watched the woman's shoes twinkling back up the path. Her hair turned out to be not so long after all: the tail was an extension reaching down from her shoulder-blades.

"Why didn't you ask her where he's gone?"

Corso turned his head to reverse, "Because she doesn't know. While we do."

"Really?"

"He packed only one case, but it was a big one, proving he was in a hurry but thought he might be away for some time. And the taxi was to take him to the airport."

"Then we have to tell our colleagues!"

"We have no mandate to do that, and in any case by now he'll be on a plane to Paris or Frankfurt. By tomorrow he'll be in South America or the Far East."

"So we're letting him get away?"

With a couple of manoeuvres, Corso got the car back onto the side road that would take them back to the main road.

"Find something to write with."

Isa pulled her computer from the pocket of her jeans.

"Seven," Corso dictated.

He drove slowly, checking the numbers on the villas to left and right along the road.

"Four," he said, "Two."

Isa entered the numbers.

At the stop sign Corso pulled up and got out of the car. Isa saw him disappear round the corner then reappear immediately afterwards, cut across the road and disappear again behind the gate of the villa facing them on the other side.

When a little later he got back into the car, she was aware again of the smell of dog that during the last month had spoilt her sleep, driving her to read a couple of books, touch herself at unusual times and no longer be able to digest certain "crutches" that until then had worked perfectly for her.

"Eighty-seven and eighty-five," Corso said, restarting the car.

Another half a dozen sharp curves and they were back amongst the city traffic. A few drops of rain had appeared on the windscreen, but the clouds gave the impression that for the time being they had no more time for rain. An oceanic sky was hanging over them, almost majestic, and the city seemed to be staring up incredulously at them, its windows and balconies open.

Corso drew up in front of a low building with windows protected by heavy bars. He stopped the engine and turned to Isa.

"The numbers I asked you to write down are the houses with C.C.T.V. on their gates. See if any of them recorded anything on December 24 last year. I know that's a long time ago and the tapes usually get thrown away or reused, but we might be lucky."

The girl stared at him, as if she could slap him.

But she controlled herself and said simply, "They don't use

tapes any more, it's all digital, not that that makes any difference. What the fuck are we looking for, anyway?"

"A C.C.T.V. recording of a stretch of road."

Isa's mobile rang where it was balanced on her thigh. She read the name of the caller and switched it off.

"This road's a dead end," Corso said. "It only has about ten numbered houses. But if we can find out which cars drove past that day, it shouldn't be difficult to know if Luda was driving one of them. It should be easy enough to make calls to the other residents and start a process of elimination."

"Fucking awful idea, and as usual, lots of extra shit for me."

Corso seemed not to be listening. He was staring at the entrance to what must once have been some sort of workshop.

"This is the only bank on the road to the villa. Might be worth having a look at their registration numbers too."

Isa turned to look. Two men in jackets and raincoats were standing at the entrance. One was very old and the other, with his leather case, spectacles and carefully parted hair, was plainly upwardly mobile.

The old man was obviously counting something, and the young one was perhaps hoping for a commission from him, or some useful experience, or maybe nothing more than the opportunity to stand beside the older man at the entrance to the bank. The old man was standing with one foot on a higher step than the other, as if to demonstrate that he really ought to be somewhere else. Probably there was nowhere else for him to be, but time had taught him that it was more effective to influence people using induction than radiation, though this is always hard work and a bore.

"So according to you, he went to Luda and Luda took him to the Cottolengo to see the Pontremoli woman?" Isa said.

Corso looked away from the two men outside the bank.

"That would explain why Luda's car was always parked there, wouldn't it?"

"Luda went to Tabasso, we've proved that. And Autumnal would have been able to take a taxi or use public transport, if he didn't want to park in that area."

"Taxis keep a record of their fares and he's not the type for buses. Besides, I think they like to do things properly.

"What the fuck does that mean?"

"Never mind." Corso said. "Where shall I drop you?"

They continued on the road to the centre, each sunk in his or her own thoughts. On the way Isa's mobile rang a couple of times. She silenced it without looking to see the caller's name, then while she was putting it into her pocket, her knee accidentally brushed Corso's hand on the gearstick. Both pretended nothing had happened. By the time they reached headquarters, a very weak sun had come out. The road was old and narrow and, looking up, at two in the afternoon, they could see a light in Arcadipane's window, the air behind it thick with smoke.

"I'll be in touch when I have something," Isa said, opening the car door.

"Can I ask you a question?"

The girl stopped. The sound of the city was coming to them through the half-open door. A modest sound, if truth be told, for a city of such size. And, as was the nature of its streets, dedicated to footsteps and the life they produced.

"Suor Luciana was furious after my visit. How did you persuade her to let you take those notebooks away?"

Isa scratched her shoulder. Two of her colleagues, at the main door, were sending them looks that were part curious and part suggestive.

"Because I know her," she said.

Corso studied Isa's irregular nose and graceful feminine neck,

and the olive skin that stretched over her collarbone before disappearing under her jacket.

"How do you know her?"

Isa looked through the window at the two colleagues, who
were now laughing openly.

"Crapheads," she said, opening the only closed button on her
jacket and pulling her shirt out of her trousers. Corso recognised
something familiar in the design tattooed on her stomach.

"That's the Madonna of Caravaggio."

"No idea," Isa said, pushing her shirt back into her trousers.
"I found it on the internet."

When she had finished adjusting her clothes they went back
to staring at what was in front of them: the main entrance to
headquarters, parked cars and shiny cobbles.

"Well? Have you nothing to say?"

"I'm a bit surprised."

A car passing close by them made the Polar shake.

"Have you never heard of the Marian Cult? I thought you
knew everything. We meet once a week to pray and talk. Nothing
special. And once a year we go to Loreto. Or would you rather
have me working for your girlfriend?"

A drop of rain fell on the windscreen. The two police officers
had gone back into the building. Corso kept one hand on the
wheel and the other on the gearstick.

"Is that where you met Suor Luciana?"

"Yes, but it doesn't mean you have to belong to the Church.
What is it to you, anyway?"

"Nothing."

"Exactly." she said, reaching for the bag between her legs.
"Anything else?"

"No."

"Then we'll be in touch."

*

Corso went into a bar on the main road.

He had often passed it before, but never stopped there. He didn't like the sign outside, or the forecourt, which was neither swept not asphalted, or the inflatable Father Christmas they had put out for the holidays. But he was in a hurry to make a call. His mobile needed charging, he had to drop by the school for a staff meeting and would be late home.

There were five tables in the bar and an alcove where a man and a woman of similar age were sitting. Not talking, just sitting. "Is there no-one here?" Corso said, after waiting for some time at the bar.

The man reacted, as he could just as well have the moment Corso came in.

"She's on her way," the man said, turning towards the woman. His glossy grey hair was combed back in fifties style, over a dark, almost Western jacket with brown lapels. The woman with him was distinguished by nothing more than a conventional permanent wave.

Corso was about to give up and go when the woman got up, crossed the room, went behind the bar and started tying on an apron. Corso noted great calm in her fingers.

"What can I get you?" the woman said when she was ready.

"A tamarind please, and I need to make a phone call."

"We can do the tamarind, but I'm not sure the phone's working. No-one uses it any more. They all have mobiles now."

"May I try?"

"Yes, but you'll need a token for five or ten."

"One for five, please."

"They don't make them anymore. As I told you, everyone has a mobile now. How much water?"

Corso looked at the finger of syrup at the bottom of the glass.

"Half and half."

"If your call is urgent," the woman said, adding the water, "we do have another telephone, but it has no meter, you just have to trust it."

"That'll do," Corso said.

"Then come with me."

The woman, like the place where he had parked his car, was neither big nor small, neither simple nor sophisticated, neither old nor good-looking, but all things considered, good enough at her job. She went ahead of him towards the corridor. They passed the man with fifties-style hair and the door to the toilets. Opposite, an opening without a door led to a storage area. The woman leaned into this and indicated something Corso could not see.

"Take your time," she said.

He waited for her steps to move away.

"It was better with the old phones," he heard the man say.

"Yes," the woman answered, "one of the things that used to be better," then he heard them sit down again noisily in the alcove. He dialled the number, feeling the cold typical of store-rooms beginning to climb his legs, something that happened when you accumulated things that need have no visual appeal.

"Hello!" it was Cesare's voice.

"It's Bramard. How are you?"

"I've got a golden wedding, the bar's full of old people, it's nearly three and I can't wait for them to go. That's how I am!"

"Elena?"

"She's here, serving the tables."

"Can I speak to her?"

"Just a minute."

Cesare put down the receiver, leaving Corso with a confused sound of voices and crockery. He came back almost at once.

"Me again. She doesn't want to talk to you."

"Busy?"

"Yes, but she doesn't want to talk anyway. She's got it in for you."

"I understand."

"Not surprising."

"What?"

"That you've understood. It's not difficult. She's got it in for you. And clearly she has her own good reasons."

"Have you been discussing it with her?"

"Of course. She talks to me. It's not me who wants her to marry an old man!"

"At one time you said it was a good idea."

"Things like that can go either way. You have to see."

"In any case, how is she?"

"Yesterday she spoke to her children on the telephone. She's calmer now. They're with their grandmother. She hasn't seen them for three months, did you know that?"

"I did."

"And that her husband's no good?"

"I had some idea of that too."

"You should think about it. She's a capable woman. Even Ombretta has noticed that."

"Ombretta?"

"The man at the tobacconist's."

"I asked you not to let her out."

"I didn't let her out. I had to go to a wedding, and you didn't want me to leave her alone, so I asked Ombretta to come in. He brought his rifle, and he's an excellent shot."

"That's not the point . . ."

"Anyway, they played cards. Ombretta says that with women of this kind . . . I'm of the same opinion. I've just got back from a wedding, and I've seen what there is around. My nephew from Savona was getting married. I was even happy about it, till I saw the bride's father"

"What's wrong with him?"

"He's a dwarf."

"So what?"

"I didn't want to be photographed beside a dwarf."

"Why not?"

Cesare hesitated. Clearly this was the first time he'd thought about it.

"I don't know, but anyway I wouldn't have it."

Corso said no more.

"What's the matter?"

"Nothing, tell Elena it won't take long, O.K.?"

"O.K. I'm not asking what you're up to."

"Thank you for that."

When he reached his uncle's house the few remaining clouds were beginning to turn red. The old man had just poured himself a plate of soup. He was still wearing his blue overalls with the logo of a producer of fertiliser, but the smell of cabbage was stronger than the smell of the stable. He set out a second plate and another glass.

During the first part of supper Corso explained what had been happening during the last few weeks, up to his call to Cesare a few hours earlier. His uncle listened in silence.

During the second part of the meal they ate cheese and said nothing. Corso needed this: he had been talking a lot that day, to more than one person and without directing the conversation. Three things he didn't like either because he wasn't used to them or vice versa.

When they had also had some nuts, his uncle got up, went

into the bedroom, and brought an old biscuit tin with some earth on it.

"You haven't told me any more," he said, "but it has occurred to me that a bit of a clean-up would do this no harm."

43

He took an unhurried breakfast with bread, margarine, Americano coffee and cereal biscuits, then allowed himself half-an-hour's t'ai chi on the terrace, almost till dawn.

The day was luminous, even if not completely clear, and the lake was barely rippled by the wind that in the morning sometimes seemed to drop altogether rather than descend by degrees from the mountains. A phenomenon that had made him immediately love the place, and the sense of cleanliness, order and renewal it brought with it.

At nine he got into his car, drove to one of the three banks where he kept a safe-deposit box, went in, cheerfully greeted the lady responsible for the semi-underground area of the bank and, once in there on his own, quickly dealt with everything.

Back in the car, he listened to a classical music radio station that was interrupted, once he crossed the frontier, by a station in the Como area transmitting real estate commercials. Turning off the radio he put on a C.D. Clémentine had sent him a few months before, with drums and a few pizzicato chords, and a woman's voice that only came in on the third track.

The Italian stretch of the autostrada, as always, turned out to be busier and more unpredictable, just like the landscape: on the Milan bypass a couple of construction sites slowed him down, and when he thought he had passed the heart of the great city, he found himself bottled up by a traffic jam a kilometre long, without any countryside to contemplate.

He changed the music to Debussy and then Satie.

The jam edged forward very slowly, until after more than an hour, Monticelli began to see signs of an incident ahead and discovered that a lane of the carriageway was closed.

Two hundred metres further on, a large articulated lorry loaded with pigs had broken the guardrail and gone into the ditch on the far side of the hard shoulder. The driver must have fallen asleep since no other vehicle seemed to have been involved. The shock when it hit the bank had been so violent that it had detached the tractor section and flung it forward another ten metres, its coupling torn apart. When Monticelli passed the scene, two patrols were trying the clear the road of dead pigs, helped by a few car drivers. The driver of the lorry was receiving first aid in an ambulance.

Monticelli lowered his window and listened to the cries of the pigs still imprisoned in the vehicle. Others were rooting in a field between the autostrada and an industrial building, unconcerned by the suffering of their fellows. Meanwhile the police and rescuers were interested in neither group, concentrating only on the carcasses lying in the road.

Monticelli found this image extremely postmodern. It made him smile. He felt in great need of another coffee, which he bought at the first Autogrill he came to, reaching the Desenzano exit at least two hours late.

He had been to the villa only once previously, many years before, but had no trouble remembering the road, just as he remembered the olives and the distant lake.

He stopped before the gate, under the gaze of two C.C.T.V. cameras, and waited for something to happen.

A man soon appeared. He had probably come from a booth

near the entrance, because Monticelli had not noticed him coming down the drive.

"Yes?"

Monticelli got out of the car and stretched his legs. "I would like to speak to the senator," he said, "but unfortunately I don't have an appointment."

The man had a shiny bald head and was wearing a pair of sunglasses too feminine for his bulk and blue suit. In any case by now the sun had almost set.

"The senator is not receiving visitors at the moment."

"Then it cannot matter that I have no appointment?"

The man thought about this, then repeated, "The senator is not receiving anyone."

"Please tell him I need to speak to him about the Sleeping Beauties."

The guard took a step towards the gate, perhaps thinking he had not heard correctly.

"I think he would not be pleased," Monticelli said, turning his back the better to see the countryside facing the villa, "if he came to know I had come all the way here for nothing."

He heard the guard's steps disappearing on the gravel. He put his hands in his pockets and waited. He preferred his own lake, though it was small, cold and irregular in shape, just as sometimes it is nicer to eat at home in comfort than to dress up and go out to a restaurant. Even the olive trees here seemed overdone. Not that he disliked them, but their air of wisdom and power was decidedly exaggerated.

When the gate opened. Monticelli got back into his car and drove up the drive.

At the other end another man very similar to the first was waiting for him, though in this case without sunglasses and dressed more like a major-domo than a bodyguard.

Monticelli got out of the car, taking with him nothing but a large envelope that had travelled on the seat beside him.

"The senator can spare you a few minutes," the man told him.

"That will be sufficient," Monticelli said.

The villa was a modest example of Palladian architecture. Its windows were open and its floors covered by expensive carpets. It had been decorated without pomp or ostentation with a few antique items and otherwise with fifties furniture: it had evidently been the home of a single long-lived family. It was silent, and from the entrance hall a flight of stairs rose to the bedrooms.

The man stopped beside a door and indicated that this was where his own territory ended. Monticelli went in.

The room, large and almost square, had walls covered with an English tapestry illustrated with rather faded flowers and a ceiling painted with rather coarse mythological hunting scenes.

Monticelli approached the wrought-iron bed in the centre of the room, watched over by another man very like the two he had already met. Also in the room were a young man in a white shirt very much with the air of being a doctor, and an older man, bent and insignificant to look at, who was busy working on a heap of papers at a desk.

There was an empty chair ready by the bedside.

Monticelli sat down.

The face of the old man lying on the bed was hidden behind an oxygen mask. Not much was left of him, apart from a few last grey hairs, two enormous ears, a sharp nose and, no doubt about it, eyes that were still pugnacious.

Looking into them, Monticelli was reminded of the embers of a fire that was once a source of light and colour, perhaps even with the power to destroy and devastate, but which now languished, capable of nothing beyond survival.

"Good evening, Senator," he said, "I don't expect you remember me."

The old man's stare indicated neither yes or no. His rising and falling chest looked as fragile as a newly baked crust of bread. A colostomy bag hung beside the bed.

"In any case," Monticelli smiled, "a mutual friend of ours has been caused a lot of bother by an old story. A series of misunderstandings, I think you'll agree."

The old man looked at one of the two men behind him.

"That being the case," Monticelli continued regardless, "I thought I'd bring you this package. A single glance will be enough for you to understand what is at stake."

The man from the writing desk approached. There were no carpets in the room, presumably to avoid dust and mites, since the condition of the occupant must have made regular airing impossible.

The man from the writing desk was wearing a cloth jacket over an old-fashioned turtleneck sweater. He took the envelope Monticelli held out to him, opened it to take a cursory look at some of the papers inside, then leaned over the old man in the bed and whispered something into his ear. Only a word or two.

Monticelli stood up and smiled.

"I'll leave this with you. I have a few copies, kept in secure places. So long as the senator stays in perfect health, that's where they will remain. Otherwise, events beyond my control will automatically make them accessible to the press and the authorities, who, as you know, are not noted for tact or reverence for old age."

He stayed standing in front of the bed long enough to be able to be sure from the eyes of the senator that he had perfectly understood everything involved.

"Take care," he concluded with a little bow, when this had been acknowledged.

*

On his way back, that evening, he left the autostrada to look for a trattoria he remembered. The place was in fact still there with its slightly modernised sign, the same wisteria on the pergola, and the familiar corner table where he had always sat.

While he waited for his plate of hot antipasti he thought he would smoke a cigar, but noticed at a nearby table a couple with a child of about two, so he held back. Above the pergola, the sky was gradually turning cobalt and the first stars were appearing in the east. The waitress was cutting bread on a trolley.

Monticelli studied her figure from behind: slender, in close-fitting blue trousers and a white blouse. But for her long black hair, she could have been mistaken for a young girl dressed for her first big social engagement.

An electric current ran down his arms and through his wrists to die at his hands.

He smiled to himself. A youthful response.

Then he took the notebook from the pocket of the jacket he had folded over the next chair and turned to the last page. He threw a tidy line through the fourth word on the list: INSUR-ANCE.

There was one still to go.

44

At the same time, two days later, Corso was climbing the stairs of a block of flats with no lift in the heart of the Porta Palazzo area of town. His instructions had been to go up to the seventh and last floor, cross the corridor and knock on the third mansard door.

Corso did so. The building, which must once have been respectable and even in rather good taste, had been allowed to go sadly downhill, judging by the rat-trap within a metre of his sandals.

He knocked and Isa opened instantly as if already waiting behind the door, and immediately turned back the way she had come.

Corso went in. On his left a steel rail held some trousers, her familiar jacket and a few shirts. A bit further in were shelves loaded with magazines, linen and T-shirts, and below them her heavy boots and a pair of work shoes.

He found Isa sitting barefoot at the table wearing a vest and man's pyjama trousers. A lamp lit the work surface and on it two computers, an electric power point and a toaster. The two mansard windows were concealed by bags of rubbish.

Hearing him behind her, the girl pulled out from under the table a "stool" the height of a box of detergent.

"Take a seat."

The box had, in fact, once contained a cleaning product called Dash.

"I've strengthened it, it won't collapse."

Corso sat down. On the table were some pistachio cream, a tube of condensed milk and a half-empty box of marron glacés.

"I'll show you," Isa said.

While she worked at the keyboard, Corso noticed her shoulders were covered with moles. These were small and dark, unlike her flesh, which at that point was otherwise clear and extremely smooth.

"I got this from the C.C.T.V. of the villa at Number 4. The others either had no archives or showed nothing but the gate."

Corso concentrated on the screen of one of the computers, which showed a sliding gate and a section of road from above, with a timer running bottom right.

When something came into the picture Isa halted it with a click.

"I've checked the model and registration," she said. "Luda's Opel. Proves he left home at 15.32 on Christmas Eve."

Corso looked more closely at the screen. He could see the doors and lower part of the windows of a small burgundy-coloured car. But only the three last digits of the rear registration plate.

"Go back a bit," he said.

The car retreated in little jumps, finally stopping when the front was visible.

Corso drew attention to a dark shadow just above the door. Isa put a marron glacé in her mouth.

"Yes, I noticed that too," she said, starting the other computer. "There's a passenger."

Corso pushed hair back from his brow. He was only now beginning to notice a smell of badly dried clothes and caramel in the room. He glanced at the posters covering the metre and a half of wall-space: concerts, a Frida Kahlo reproduction, the enlarged photograph of a cell, the Madonna tattooed on Isa's belly and several motorcycles ridden by half-naked blonde women in sunglasses.

"Trying to work this out," Isa said, "I nearly ruined my eyes."

Corso turned to the other screen, which she had just switched on.

"From seven that morning to three thirty, which is roughly when Luda set off with his passenger for the city, thirteen cars passed on that road. None of the registrations can be seen complete, but I've compared the ones which can be read with the makes of the cars and telephoned the residents to check them: four turned out to belong to residents and seven to people visiting them. So the remaining two can only have gone to Luda's house."

The timer at the base of the picture began to run and after a few seconds a white car appeared, in this case too with only its lower part visible. When Isa stopped the film, the timer showed 10.32 and fifteen seconds.

"This is a Fiorino, and its three visible registration numbers led me to a maintenance firm. When I called them they confirmed they went to Luda that morning to fix his electric gate. Which apparently wouldn't open properly. The job took them an hour at most: I checked and in fact the Fiorino passed by again towards midday."

Isa clicked a couple of keys. The screen went dark, then went back to showing the gate and the road.

"But the car coming next is the mystery one."

The timer started at 13.06. A moment later a dark car crossed the picture heading up the road. Isa stopped the picture at 13.06 and thirty-eight seconds. As with the Fiorino, the car's doors could be seen, with part of its rear registration plate and a corner of its windscreen.

"Is that an Audi?"

"Yes, an A6 or maybe an A8. You can only read the last three numbers and then there's that other thing . . ."

Corso leaned his elbows on his knees for a closer look.

"Can you enlarge it?"

"A bit, but it just disintegrates. See? Could be a leaf or a stain."

Corso noticed a movement on his right.

A girl's face suddenly appeared from under a duvet. Her eyes were half shut but she seemed about to get up, then gave a groan and fell back, her face a mess of mascara round a swollen lip.

"What happened to her?"

Isa had not taken her eyes off the screen.

"I don't know," was all she said. "She came back like that."

"Perhaps you ought to take her to hospital?"

"Fuck the girl, I told her to keep away from that rave." She put another marron glacé in her mouth. "As far as I'm concerned that's not a leaf, but it's not a stain either."

Corso stared at the other girl again: the smell of caramel seemed to be coming from her. Then he turned back to the dark car and whatever was to the right of the registration numbers.

"Go back a bit."

"But then we won't be able to see the registration plate anymore!"

"I know, stop on the door."

Isa did this.

Corso propped one elbow on the table.

"Can you see that square thing on the windscreen?"

"Yes," Isa said. "What is it? A reflection?"

"Can you look up the registration system for Swiss cars?"

Isa stopped a moment with her fingers suspended over the

keys, then began tapping again. A page of Swiss car registrations appeared.

"So what you get is numbers followed by the arms of the canton," Corso said.

"So what?"

"That thing on the windscreen could be the *vignette*."

"What's that?"

"It's a sticker they have to show on motorways in Switzerland. If the car has a *vignette*, and something that looks like a sticker after the registration number, it could be a sign that it's registered in Switzerland."

As she studied this, Isa's concentration and concern matched his own. It was only now that he suddenly understood, for the first time, the nature of the bitterness she could not escape and that forced her to be so defensive every time she opened her mouth.

"Even if that's true," was all she said now, "you can't tell which coat of arms it is."

Corso pointed to something on the left of the page.

"Are those the arms of the cantons?"

"Yes."

"The one on the registration plate seems uncoloured. If we cut out the coloured ones how many does that leave us?"

Isa ran her eyes over the two columns of symbols.

"Four," she said. "Or possibly five."

Corso got up and pushed his hands into his pockets intending to take a few paces round the table, but on the far side the floor was covered with electric cables and the ceiling was too low. He stopped and lowered his head.

"So we have a blue Audi with three registration numbers visible, and it comes from one of those five cantons," he said. "Do you think we can get there?"

Isa gave him a longer stare than she ever had ever given him before.

Suddenly the other girl let out a noise like a blind and defenceless puppy trying to say "please".

Isa gave her a casual glance.

"Was that not her?"

Corso shook his head to indicate no, albeit a somewhat complex no.

Isa looked down at the small plate riveted to the arm of her chair that proclaimed it to be Police property. She fussed at the plate with her tape-bound thumbnail and shrugged.

"Not me either."

As Corso got up to go, she took the last marron glacè from the box, pushed it into her mouth, and got back to work.

45

The day had been characterised since dawn by a gentle sunlight that the clouds occasionally touched but never covered. A long, full June day, with no unexpected rain or wind. When at nine that evening Cesare came into the kitchen and sat down at the table set for two, the atmosphere that surrounded the old things in the room was still warm and promising.

"How did it go?" he asked.

Elena was mixing what smelt of egg, garlic and salt in a frying pan with a wooden spoon. She had noticed the presence of the old man, as she always noticed everything without showing it. The very first thing Cesare came to value in her was that she never wasted words.

"Alright," she said. "Nothing in particular."

Cesare cut two slices of bread and put them near their plates, while Elena brought over the frying pan and a saucepan.

"Wine?" he said.

She nodded, dividing the omelette in four. Her hair was pulled back in a ponytail, the way it always was when they were working in the bar. The only time he ever saw it loose was in the morning, when they shared an early breakfast.

"He didn't carry you off to make a pass, did he? Because that man . . ." Cesare waved an expressive hand beside his head.

Elena said no. She served Cesare some omelette, together with two spoonfuls of vegetables, and put the same amount on her own plate.

"We went up on a hill."

"Lis?"

They were both sitting down by now.

"No."

"Battagliola?"

"It could have been Battagliola."

Cesare took a mouthful of omelette, together with a piece of black bread he had broken off with his fingers. Garlic showed white among the green vegetables.

"Do you know what this is called?" he said.

Elena was eating too. She shook her head.

"*Rugnusa.* I always make it on days when we're closed. I put in everything that's been left in the bar. But you've done it well, better than me."

Elena nodded at the vegetables.

"It's extremely good, what's in it beside the beet?"

"Garlic, anchovies."

"Excellent," Cesare confirmed. "Did you tell him?"

Elena drank some wine.

"I told him I'll go and talk to that gentleman when I come back."

"And what did he say to that?"

She shrugged.

Cesare massaged his right leg. During the changeable seasons it gave him pain so he went on wearing corduroy till high summer: age had taught him not to let his enthusiasms run away with him.

"He could at least have come in," he said. "I had some books to give him."

"Some woman telephoned him. He said he had to go back at once."

229

"Who telephoned him?"

"I don't know, a police colleague, I think."

Cesare looked at Elena, her beauty as calm and relaxed as that of Saint Barbara, then at the window overlooking the road. Once those who worked in the valley were home, the whole night could slip by without a single further car passing.

"I've known him thirty years," he said. "Not many have his intelligence and warm heart, but he's not made for other people. Maybe that could have been changed if his wife . . . but after what happened. I got like that myself after Adele died. That's why he and I get on, but for someone else . . . More wine?"

Elena indicated that she'd had enough. Cesare filled his own glass again, then put down the bottle, and they went on eating in silence as earlier, though then they had eaten downstairs among the last afternoon customers and those early for dinner.

The bar had no particular opening or closing times. Cesare would decide such things on the spur of the moment according to how he felt. Last Saturday and Sunday there had been a golden wedding and a Confirmation party, not to mention the holidaymakers who had begun to arrive with the good weather, so after the weekend he had kept the bar closed for two days. No-one had telephoned to make a booking and he was not beholden to casual passers-by. No harm done. He saw this as his last year, after which he would close down, not passing the bar or even the licence on to anyone else. He was seventy-three now, his dog was in poor health and he had no intention of getting another. Nor did he have any children, and a bar without children or a decent dog was nothing.

What if a woman like Elena had come to him rather than to that other man?

He had given some thought to that: the idea of having her to work with him and having her living there too: only for company, of course, because after a certain age it's better not to risk making a fool of yourself, but in the end, despite how much he liked the woman, not even that would have persuaded him to keep the bar going. He had decided to retire after this summer at the latest. But he would go on living above the premises, looking after the garden, borrowing more books from Corso and spending more time watching television. There were so many channels he knew nothing about. Now he would have time to study them. He might still rent out the bar to the Alpini or the Red Cross for special events if they asked him. But he would leave them to it, without even coming down to see what they were up to. Let them just get on with it, they had their own people to do the cooking and serving. He would stay upstairs. Or they could ask the Church for help.

"Did you know his wife?"

It took Cesare a little time to come back from his thoughts. Meanwhile Elena had cleaned her plate. She ate plenty and quickly, like all people who see eating as a practical function.

"I saw her once or twice," he said, "but at that time he used to come here less often and almost always alone."

"What was she like?"

Cesare helped himself to more omelette.

"French." He shrugged. "I've never liked the French. Particularly not the men, a lazy lot, but not the women either . . . And when they did come together, she mostly talked to Adele. Adele spoke well of her, but then Adele always had a good word for everyone. She even got the priest to come up here and bless her secretly so as not to get on the wrong side of her husband. I think she was a schoolteacher. But that doesn't necessarily mean . . ."

He got up and took his plate to the sink. They took turns

washing up and this evening it was his turn. He had a dish-washer but never used it, he didn't like the noise. But first he put a bottle of Genepì and two small cups on the table.

"Do you think he's got himself into some sort of mess?" he said, sitting down again.

Elena said she didn't know and went on eating.

Cesare poured himself a finger of the Genepì Corso had picked the previous summer and which he, Cesare, had steeped in alcohol and filtered. It smelt good and was also good for the digestion. He poured a finger for Elena as well.

"This evening there's camel-racing at Dubai," he said. "If that's of any interest to you."

46

"Which is he?"

"Number 25."

"25 red or white?"

"Red, fuck it, the one who . . . just attempted that sod-awful pass!"

Corso watched a short stocky boy plodding along behind a tall thin one who had just snatched the ball from him. It seemed such an effort for him to have to move on such stumpy legs, yet his adolescent face was etched with unflappable determination. The game was clearly no pleasure to him, just the primitive duty of one who knows he must suffer to succeed. In fact, he now managed to extract the ball from the feet of the tall thin one and pass it to a teammate, another who like the tall thin one belonged to the category of those who might equally happily and effortlessly either let the ball go or hang on to it and achieve something memorable.

Corso's jacket was tight on his shoulders. He unbuttoned it. The cloudy morning did not threaten rain; it was just that the sun, quite simply, seemed determined to spend the day behind clouds. The thermometer on the front of the chemist's shop opposite the sports ground showed 19 degrees.

"You see that one?" Arcadipane said.

"The one with long hair?"

"Never mind his hair," the commissario said irritably. "In a couple of seasons that boy will be playing in Serie A. Tiracini – remember the name, you'll see I'm right."

"I'll remember. Any news?"

"Turn!" he shouted, "Turn!" his body as tense as if he were one of only two defenders left to face a sudden counter-attack.

Among the hundred or so people perched on the rough concrete terraces, it was mainly the fathers who were shouting. Most of the mothers restricted themselves to occasionally interrupting their chatter to applaud or show restrained disappointment. Corso had always hated football, especially watching it. The only things he remembered as worse were going to the shooting range for compulsory gun practice, reading the horoscope, and having to wait a long time for his food. Arcadipane, on the other hand, even when he was Corso's deputy, had allowed himself half an hour every morning to discuss the football headlines in *Gazzetta dello Sport* with his colleagues. Like most southern Italians, he was a Juventus supporter, and like most Italians it caused him no embarrassment at all that his son played for a club affiliated to the rival outfit, Torino.

"Great, fuck it! Great!" he sneered loudly, "Don't pass! Don't pass!" then sat down again, big hands spread on his knees. Other parents were settling too, and the women had gone back to their chatter.

"Well?" Corso said.

Arcadipane stopped a moment with his mouth open, but the drama ended in banality with a corner kick.

"Luda's in Cambodia," he admitted unwillingly, "but because no-one there reads or writes we have no extradition agreement with them. As for the other thing, we argued three days with the Greeks, only to find there was no D.N.A. to be found: just an empty coffin."

Corso passed a finger through his beard. He knew Arcadipane had been totally obsessed for several days with tracking down Luda and putting pressure on the Greeks to allow Pontremoli's brother to be exhumed. And that since his telephone call the previous evening he had been desperate to find out what Corso had to tell him. But he would just have to imagine it: no small hairy southerner could afford to seem too zealous, particularly in the police.

"Well?" the commissario goaded him. "Do we have to bugger ourselves over this even on a Saturday?"

Corso took a sucai from his pocket and put it in his mouth.

"Remember the C.C.T.V. idea?"

"Utter crap."

"Well, we have a name and address."

"Who's we?"

"Isa and me, for the moment."

Arcadipane watched with disproportionate interest as a small boy in red placed the ball beside the corner flag. The sun seemed almost to have changed its mind about coming out: perhaps the afternoon would be different.

"So now you've started holding back information from the authorities?" he asked.

The small boy took a few steps back. With his long fair hair he looked like a woman recovering from a long illness.

"The truth is," Corso said, "I've come to watch the son of a friend play football."

"Glad to hear it." Arcadipane scratched his thigh. "Because if this had been an official conversation, it would have been my duty to remind you that as a member of the public it is your duty to pass on all useful information to the police. And if a public official discovers that you are not intending to do this, it is his duty to set in motion all the measures at his disposal, including arrest or other precautionary measures, so as to avoid enquiries being hindered or the law being broken or even graver crimes."

The small blond boy kicked the ball. There was a dull violent thud not commensurate with the slenderness of the kicker, which caused six or seven players to leap into the air together and one, jumping higher than the others, to succeed in changing the direction of the ball, which struck the ground first, then a post, then finally finished up in the net. Half the spectators leaped to their feet in celebration.

"And what if this were not an official conversation?" Corso said.

Arcadipane took a pack of Muratti cigarettes from his pocket, stuck one between his lips and lit it. The players in red hugged the tall thin boy who had put the ball in the net.

"In that case I'd tell you it was all a load of crap and that wouldn't make you feel any better."

Corso watched Arcadipane's son move back to his own side of the field with his teammates. It would be idiotic to say he had grown. It was ten years since Corso had last seen him and in ten years a child doesn't just grow: he comes to exist.

"Then it's a good thing I only came to watch Luca play," he said.

Arcadipane watched his son pursue an adversary along the touchline, survive a tackle, send the ball into touch, get to his feet again, straighten a shin-guard and go back to his position.

"Bless his two little bollocks!" the affectionate father said. "But if only the lad could grow another couple of centimetres!"

47

Jean-Claude Monticelli opened the sliding door and went into the room.

The space was basic: a coir mat, fabric-lined walls, a low ceiling of light-coloured wood and, beyond the window, an intensely dark night, barely touched by light reflected from the lake.

He turned on the standard lamp. On the table, which was a platform of boards resting on metal trestles, a dozen bonsais were set out in a semicircle.

He sat down, and taking a pair of silver-mounted spectacles from the pocket of the shirt he was wearing loose outside his trousers, began scrutinising the plants as calmly as a man of rank would once have assessed village girls assembled for his pleasure in the courtyard of his manor. Finally he pulled towards him a *ficus benjamina* from his right.

He considered its branches, its dimensions and its colour, then tested the soil first with his fingers, then with a hollow needle. When he had finished, he cleaned the needle with a cloth and stood up. Some cheap shelving held an old box made of dark wood and a high-tech audio system of the same colour. Opening the box, Monticelli took out a roll of velvet, switched on the stereo and went back to the table.

Monticelli unlaced the package, which revealed laid out against the blue velvet some twenty shining instruments: pincers, shears, scalpels, blades and saws, all so small as to make one think of tools for making ships to go into bottles.

Monticelli extracted the *ficus* from its pot firmly but with great care. He cleaned all the soil from its roots with a fine brush, cut it where he thought it necessary and, putting it back in the pot, began to surround it with fresh soil.

"People think nature follows a vision of perfection," he said, "but that's not how it is."

He pushed the *ficus* aside and turned towards Corso, who was watching him from the door with arms down by his sides and the Luger in his left hand.

"That's why some of us are here." Monticelli was smiling. "To bear witness to a beauty that demands to be set free!"

Turning back to the table, he took another bonsai out of its pot and began to clean its roots just as he had with the first.

"It isn't work that requires much effort, let's be honest about that. Beauty almost always hides behind a thin membrane. You need to take away very little and you should add even less, but you must be confident enough to do the right thing at the right time."

Taking one of the larger pincers, he pruned a root showing signs of rot.

"It's no use waiting for everyone to understand this fact. Most people run to museums to see the paintings of Van Gogh, but deep down they still write him off as a mentally sick man who cut off his own ear, made those close to him suffer, and whose paintings were gross and infantile. But you understood from the first. It can't be painless, pain is often inevitable, but you have understood that. That's why it has been so stimulating in recent years to be able to hold this dialogue with you."

The water outside the window was disturbed by a passing boat, making the reflected lights dance to a more vibrant rhythm.

Corso watched the water gradually settle down again, after which the window gave him once more the image of a man in a white shirt, calm, lucid and intent on caring for a small plant, and behind him the image of another man, hardened and tired, with hair too long for his age and a weapon in his left hand.

"You have many doubts," Monticelli nodded, looking back at the glass, "which is why you are here. You didn't come for revenge or out of a sense of justice as you have tried to make everyone believe. In fact your questions only have one answer. Did what happened, happen in the name of beauty? And did it produce a beauty greater than the sacrifice involved? The answer is yes."

He stopped working on the bonsai and pushed it aside.

"Of course you can look for other reasons if you want to, but if you do you'll just find yourself back in the desert where most people walk. A waste and a humiliation for minds of the quality of yours and mine."

A bleep sounded in the house: a short, discreet, regular signal.

Monticelli stood up. Corso, as if his arm were linked to the man's body by a thread, lifted the Luger. Monticelli stopped.

"May I?"

Corso gazed at the man's cold but sad eyes: the firmness he saw in them reminding him of the images of certain pagan kings depicted in churches to commemorate their simultaneous acts of cruelty and mercy. The signal continued, monotonous and sleepy, too faint to drown the song.

Corso stepped backwards, holding the gun high. Monticelli turned the volume of the stereo down and moved towards the door. When he passed through it, the barrel of the Luger nearly touched his temple. Corso continued to hold him in his sights as he went to the desk in the next room, switched on a lamp and sat down at a computer.

"I thought you'd stood me up!" said a young woman's voice.

Monticelli smiled, his face reflected in the light from the computer screen.

"I'd never do that," he said. "How did it go?"

"So-so. One of the women has decided to leave the programme. Seems her husband forced her to. Sheila says in cases like this it's better not to insist, which would be worse."

"She could be right."

"I know, but it makes me sick."

"You can't do everything yourself. Africa's a big place."

Corso was aware that the woman talking to Monticelli must be smiling, though he could not see her.

"Are you listening to music?" she said.

"Yes."

"Classical or Cohen?"

"Cohen."

"I miss that, you know?"

"But you hated it!"

"Then let's say I miss standing there with you looking at the lake, despite the music."

"Liar! You were dying of boredom. Like the lake."

They laughed. Corso saw that Monticelli had perfect teeth. In the days when he had a lot of interrogating to do he had noticed a relationship between self-command and teeth, and had written his observations down in a notebook. Burned now.

"When are you going into the city?" Monticelli said.

"I don't know," the girl said. "There should be some material arriving Tuesday or Wednesday, but it's not certain."

"Drop by the hotel, you'll find a letter there."

"From you?"

"Yes. In the envelope there's an air ticket in your name. I need you back for a few days at the end of the month."

"What's going on?"

"Nothing. All is explained in the letter."

"Why not tell me now? You just make me worry otherwise."

Monticelli moved the video camera from the top of the screen where it had been perched.

"What are you doing?" the girl said. "Why have you moved it?"

"Wait," Monticelli said. "I'm going to prop the camera somewhere else." He put it turned towards himself on top of a pile of books on Chinese art. "Can you see me?"

"Yes, but what's the matter with you? You're strange this evening!"

Monticelli turned the computer so Corso could see the screen too.

"Nothing's the matter," he said. "I'm no more strange than usual."

Corso studied the girl, beautiful with the simple beauty of twenty years. She had short hair, green eyes and an imperfect mouth, and her cheeks were still full. Slightly prominent cheekbones were the only evidence that she was already an adult, capable of giving as well as taking, already dangerous.

"Why are you being so mysterious?" the girl asked. "What's in the letter?"

"Nothing for you to worry about," Monticelli said. "I mention a friend in it."

"What friend?"

Monticelli looked at Corso.

"Papà?"

The two men stared at each other.

"Papà?"

"Yes," Monticelli said, looking back into the video camera. "You haven't turned gay, have you?"

"No," Monticelli smiled. "No, I haven't changed course."

The girl smiled too before turning to one side, perhaps to check no-one was watching her, and stroked the curve of her neck.

A long electric impulse shot through Corso's legs.

One evening, many years before, he had been sitting with Michelle outside their tent on the beach on an island in the Tyrrhenian Sea. It was nearly dark, they were young and laughing and Michelle had turned to look at a cane fence, an unpoetic palisade, a mere windbreak. Then she had lifted her hand and stroked her neck. The same light touch, the same profile.

The Luger was infinitely heavy in Corso's hand. He leaned against the doorpost so as not to have to lower it.

"I think you've been drinking this evening." The girl smiled again, wiping an eye with the back of her hand.

"A bit," Monticelli agreed. "But I've got to go now. I give you a big hug."

"Sure everything's alright, Papà?"

"Sure . . ." Monticelli smiled, and for the first time there was a catch in his voice, "Remember I love you."

She laughed. "I'll be sure to remember."

"Kiss you."

"Kiss you."

Corso saw the screen go dark as the girl lifted her fingers to her lips. An instant later it was black. Leonard Cohen's voice was no longer filling the room, but Corso could not have said when it stopped.

"Let's go and sit outside," Monticelli said. "We both need a drink."

48

He found Monticelli stretched out on one of two chaises longues, his hands behind his head and his eyes turned to the black mass of the lake. Between the chairs, a small table held two glasses, a bundle wrapped in cloth, an envelope and a bottle.

Corso approached.

Monticelli poured a finger of brandy into each of the glasses. The light from the lamp in the room behind them was cutting across his face.

"Sit," he said.

Corso remained standing. He could hear the lake, which seemed to be crouching beneath them like an agile and dangerous animal.

"We've been waiting a long time for this meeting," Monticelli said, "so, if you agree, I'd rather not waste it on banalities. We both know that with money one can be dead while still alive, can cultivate one's preferred vices with discretion and even have children attributed to oneself that one has not fathered."

Corso looked at the hills and then at the mountains, where the black matched the black of the sky.

"What does she know?"

"Clémentine?"

"Martina."

"Of course, Martina," Monticelli conceded with a vague gesture.

"She knows her mother died just after she was born and that I took over looking after her. It has been stimulating to create the life of a wife one never had. To provide a few family friends and photographs, and the odd distant relative."

Corso pointed the Luger at him. Monticelli lifted the glass to his lips and took a sip of brandy.

"Not yet." he said, putting the glass back on the table. Then he took the envelope and threw it on the empty chair.

"Here are the keys to the cellar. You'll find five cylinders full of gas and an old gas ring, All you have to do is light the ring and open the cylinders. You'll have four minutes to get to your car and be off. I've spread some cans of petrol round the house to make sure the job is done properly. Explosions are never predictable."

He stopped to swallow a little more brandy.

"As for an investigation," he smacked his lips, "don't give that a thought. A doctor and a lawyer hold case reports that confirm the advanced state of my illness. They will release them to the investigators. My act, though tragic, will appear perfectly rational. I have left instructions for my property to pass to Clém . . . to Martina," he corrected himself. "It will be a satisfactory inheritance. I also speak of you in the letter as an old friend they can consult."

He emptied the glass and turned to search for Corso's eyes above the Luger.

"Of course, if you decide to explain everything to her, the D.N.A. will prove you right, but I think she will prefer not to know who the man who brought her up and loves her like a father really was. So, Commissario Bramard, my advice"– and he reached out a hand to open the cloth package that contained his pistol – "is to light the gas ring and go and enjoy your daughter, even if she never finds out who she is."

"Stop!" shouted Corso.

Monticelli took a deep breath of the night air and released it slowly.

"In that envelope," he said, indicating the table, "there's a photograph of someone you don't know, but whose death may make things easier for someone you care for. And as far as the Snoring Beauties are concerned, I've made sure no-one will bother you further about them. Accept these things as a present from me in return for all the years you've had to spend chasing me. It's been a tremendous match."

"If that hair hadn't been in the envelope I wouldn't be here now."

Monticelli shrugged.

"A small concession. Up till then I always had the advantage. In the end the only thing that ever matters is beauty, and you have enabled me to live a wonderful life."

Then he lifted the Beretta to his temple and fired.

Corso lowered the Luger and stared at the red trail Monticelli's head was leaving on the chaise longue as he slipped to one side with theatrical slowness. A woman he had loved, a daughter he had lost and twenty years of investigation, all in that red stain that would oxidise, darken and cool.

He crouched on his haunches and watched the lake sloshing around under the planks of the floor, then picked up the envelope.

It contained the key, a polaroid photograph and a ticket marked with date, name of airport and time of arrival. The polaroid showed a man with a bullet in his forehead.

"Good God! Adrian!" Corso said, seeing the Romanian newspaper on the man's chest.

He went back into the house. On the upper floor were two bedrooms, both overlooking the lake. One room had only bare essentials: a futon, low cherry-wood furniture, small modern sculptures and Chinese prints on the walls. But the other bore traces of a recent adolescence: Nirvana, Freud, Che Guevara, Franco Basaglia, Martin Luther King and Patti Smith, lots of C.D.s, two notebooks and shelves with schoolbooks, university lecture notes and photograph albums.

Corso nearly took one, then decided no.

He glanced at the five-litre jerrycan in the middle of the parquet floor, similar to one he had seen on the stairs, and went out.

He had no trouble finding the room in the cellar and opening its metal door with the key. Inside were the gas cylinders and a gas ring for camping and, on the walls, on enormous rigid panels, photographs of the six women, the black and white of their backs incised as for a funeral rite that might serve as a sophisticated passport to Hades. There was nothing else, except a lighter beside the gas ring.

He sat on the floor against the concrete wall, listening to the leaves murmur in the courtyard close outside the windows. He listened for a long time, considering the two roads open to him, one fast and the other complicated; one allowing silence and the other inevitably demanding a huge quantity of words.

Far away, a night bird began to sing, and in its monotonous lament Corso recognised his last twenty years, passed in a room like the one he was in now, the backs of those women always before his eyes, cold concrete in his bones and a bomb as an alternative in the middle of the room.

Then, like a prisoner horrified to realise that he is beginning to prefer being inside to being outside, he got up unsteadily, left the cellar and climbed the stairs.

He found the telephone and dialled the number. In a frame on the desk was the image of a thirteen-year-old, not the girl he had seen that evening on the screen, but on the way to becoming her. Beside the writing paper, a Montblanc pen.

After three rings, Arcadipane answered.

"Yes?"

"Corso here."

Silence. Then a woman's voice. "Who is it?"

"Nothing, go to sleep, I'll take it in the other room."

Footsteps. A door closing. Silence.

"Corso?"

"Yes."

"Have you been doing what you shouldn't have been doing?"

"I don't think so."

"O.K., call the Swiss Police, if such a thing exists. I'll send someone at once."

49

Monica slipped a cigarette out of the packet she had been holding in her hand all this time and lit it. Her first mouthful of smoke climbed the stairs of the fire escape where they had taken refuge.

"I don't know what to say. This thing is . . ." Hearing steps coming up the stairs she interrupted herself.

It was two girls from the Fourth, one fat and the other carrying the book for the driving-test quiz under her arm.

When they saw Monica and Corso the girls hid their cigarettes in the palms of their hands and passed between the two teachers as if in danger of being pricked by a couple of cactuses.

"This is a fire escape, bloody hell!" Monica shouted after them. "I'll report you to the head and you'll get a fine!"

The steps climbed faster to the door on the floor above, which the students kept open by sticking a pen in the latch.

"Just fuck off!" came a whisper as the door closed.

"Cows!" Monica called, then took a couple of pulls without taking the filter from her lips.

"I want to ask you millions of things, but I suppose for the moment I'll have to be satisfied with what you've already told me."

"I think so."

"Because among other things that's already something . . ."

"Enough."

"You can't do everything the first day, can you?"

Corso nodded.

"O.K.," she said, throwing her cigarette away.

"They climbed to the top floor, where Monica had jammed the door open with a hairpin. Once inside she put it back in her hair, put her hand over her face and began to sob.

"Sorry," she said. "I must seem so stupid. You're the one who should be disturbed, but instead . . ."

She mopped her cheeks. Meanwhile the bell rang.

"But there's one thing I must ask you, if I can," he said.

"O.K."

"Promise you won't be angry?"

"I won't be angry."

"When you go to the airport . . ." she hesitated, watching him. "Because you will be going to the airport, won't you? Don't decide anything now, I do understand that, but I mean, if you don't feel like going on your own, remember you can ask me, O.K.? To come with you, I mean. At any time. Even just five minutes beforehand, O.K.?"

"I'll think about it," Corso said, "At the moment I'm . . ."

"Of course! How could you not feel confused! I don't even know how you can be here at all. In your place I would have been completely knocked out by fright and happiness and everything else. I wouldn't even be able to . . ."

She stopped, waving her hands in the air at a loss for words, then flung her arms round his neck and hugged him.

Corso raised his own hands rather more timidly till he felt her back shaking with sobs under his fingers. During the time he remained like this, his collar wet with her tears, it seemed to him that something buried for many years had come to the surface, not perhaps quite intact but at least still functioning.

"The bell's gone," he said eventually.

"I know." Monica loosened her embrace and tried to tidy the make-up on her cheeks with a small paper tissue, making it worse. Realising this she laughed, at the same time still crying a little and lifting her nose in the air.

"Oh well!" She screwed the tissue into a ball. "I have some updates on the Lafleur case. Want to hear?"

"Only if it's good news."

"Her people have finally had her waxed and her swimming friends don't tease her anymore."

"Good, and the catch?"

Monica shrugged.

"They're marrying her off in a couple of months and we've been asked to the wedding."

All the students were perched on the windowsills in his classroom. The only ones sitting in their places were two girls interested only in chattering over some sheet of paper scrawled on in pencil. And a boy and girl quarrelling near the empty coat hangers. She had a big bust and he had curly hair: they were twins.

Corso sat down at the teacher's desk, opened the register and began the register, forcing the rest to converge on their places like a herd of animals.

When they were all seated, Corso got up and went to look out of the window.

In the road, a boy was looking at the school with his back against one of the plane trees. His trousers were dirty with lime and he was wearing steel toecaps. Corso remembered him two years before with the others in the corridors.

"Are we doing History or Italian first?" someone wanted to know.

Corso continued to stare at the boy leaning against the tree: he seemed to be greeting the building.

"Annarumma," he said. "What can you tell me about the picture we looked at in the book last time?"

The girl he addressed slid her mobile phone under the desk and took the book from her neighbour.

While she was trying to find the page, Corso was listening to a sound he had been aware of ever since the first day he had faced a class. He had spent many years trying to place it, but now he knew it was made by students who had been forced to push thoughts meaningful to them into a corner of their minds so as to make room for thoughts forced upon them by others. It was something like the wail or whimper of a large automatic gate with a stone stuck in its mechanism jamming it.

"Basically," Annarumma started, "in Spain there were communists and Hitler didn't like them, so he decided to bomb them and use force to destroy them. Basically, the painter was there during the bombardment and painted the place as it was afterwards, in fact showing a woman with a dead child and pieces of bodies, and a horse and a bull which means bull-fighting, and a light-bulb which is a symbol of progress."

Corso watched the boy's back now moving away down the avenue towards the building site. In the primary school opposite, a woman was writing on a blackboard and turning every now and then to face the children. It seemed to Corso that her hands must be moving in time with some kind of music.

"But if you found yourself in front of that picture what would you think?" he said to Annarumma.

"You'd have to see how big it is."

Someone laughed.

"It's about four times the size of this blackboard," Corso said. The primary school teacher had stopped writing and was

251

walking among the children who were bent over their exercise books. Passing near the window, Corso recognised a woman he sometimes saw waiting for the bus in the shelter. A dry, rather grey woman, whom he now found beautiful.

"If it's as big as that," Annarumma said, "perhaps I'd think bombs are ugly, but also that after all life has to go on."

Corso waited for the hubbub in the class to die down and listened for the wailing gate.

Realising he could not hear it, he nodded at Annarumma. Then, taking his hands out of his pockets, he picked up a piece of chalk he had left on the windowsill three days before, and went to the blackboard.

50

Two hours later he was ordering rare meat and a half-litre of wine in a restaurant he always passed on his way home. Faced with an empty plate he discovered an unexpected hunger, and asked for some rice and mushrooms.

While he was eating, together with two workmen, a couple and a lorry driver, the proprietress was sorting dispatch notes. Corso studied her tired-looking arms, her apron and tied-back hair, her still taut if now lower-slung breasts and other evidence of the passing of time.

She had been his first lover, thirty-five years before.

He could remember the rustle of grass against his trousers that evening, distant music from a country festival. She had been wearing a shirt that might almost have come from London, and was working for a firm that producing pasta and tinned food. He had been in his second year at university then, and had not told anyone that he had applied for the police. The girl did not like uniforms, so it was just as well she did not know.

They had already been studying each other for several weeks, each increasingly curious to discover what the other was like under his or her clothes. They spent one whole summer together. But when they saw each other again that autumn in a cinema queue, when Corso was in uniform and she with the man now in the restaurant kitchen, they had spoken to each other like strangers.

Now when Corso went to the counter and paid, they exchanged the informal "ciao" they had relearned with time.

The sky outside was like a grey coastline full of inlets. It was probably going to rain. He headed for the telephone in a corner of the parking area, put in two coins and dialled the number.

Then waited.

"Elena?"

DAVIDE LONGO was born in 1971 in the province of Torino, Italy. He is a writer, documentary film-maker and teacher of creative writing at the Scuola Holden in Turin. His first novel in English translation, *The Last Man Standing*, was published by MacLehose Press in 2012 to widespread critical acclaim. *Bramard's Case* is the first of a series of crime novels featuring Commissario Corso Bramard.

SILVESTER MAZZARELLA has been translating Swedish and Italian literature professionally since 1997. He learned English from his mother, Italian from his father, and Swedish in Finland, where he taught English for many years at the University of Helsinki. He now lives in Canterbury, England.